SODOM AND BEGORRAH

The True Story of the Irish—Iraq War

To Paul
My fellow Ribo111ster

Nov 2017

SODOM AND BEGORRAH

The True Story of the Irish–Iraq War

With best wishes

Ian Williams

Ian Williams

The Book Guild Ltd.
Sussex, England

This book is dedicated to
Cati, Ashley, Ceri, their grandparents and the five beautiful
ladies who have spent more than a few nights with me.

The Book Guild Ltd.
25 High Street,
Lewes, Sussex

First published 1994
© Ian Williams 1994
Set in Baskerville
Typesetting by Acorn Bookwork,
Salisbury, Wiltshire
Printed in Great Britain by
Antony Rowe Ltd.
Chippenham, Wiltshire.

A catalogue record for this book is available from the British Library

ISBN 0 86332 926 8

PART I
YESTERDAY

1

The party was in full swing in Room 209 of the Al-Rashid
Hotel, Baghdad. The Irish were getting down to the serious
business of relaxing after a hard day at the hospital. A con-
stant stream of Ferida crates appeared via room service,
bills were signed with gay abandon by whoever was nearest
the door. Dire Straits throbbed on.

In one corner laments were starting, whilst in the adjoining bedroom two consultant surgeons competed against
each other in the standing long jump from one bed to
another. Inevitably the widening gap eventually foiled them
and more Ferida flowed onto the specially made, best-
money-can-buy carpets. Unfortunately at that time they
had nowhere else to put the Irish.

Watching this scene was a recently arrived surgeon, the
token Englishman on the staff; reverse discrimination. A
veteran of bars all over the world, he was fortyish, growing
to fat around the waist and thin around the crown. He
soon noticed the pretty blond, but also took in the look of
fierce contempt as she dismissed his Englishness and continued her lament of yet another bloody Irish hero leaving
Erin's shore. He turned his attention to his new colleague,
O'Sliven, who was pontificating on the merits of Cork football at the same time pounding his Ferida bottle on to the
window sill. He looked surprised when he was left with only
half a bottle and wet feet.

England had flown in that day from Saudi Arabia, looking for something better, and adjourned immediately to the bar where the boys and girls were gathering for the night's entertainment. He'd witnessed the deputy matron, a lady of formidable proportions, walk out of the somewhat dimly lit bar, a sop to Moslem sensitivities, straight into the adjoining fountain. A few brave souls waded in to drag her out and leave her gasping for air, like a beached whale. Some said she had been gin and tonicked on arrival, others pondered the role of senior nurses, but then there are always others.

England left the fag end of the party and lumbered along to his room, two down. He expected noise, but the hotel was built to last. It was said that if a bomb went off in one room, next door would be intact. With the Irish this was a great boon. They had also lent their name to the concrete shields outside each window which were designed to deflect bombs. They had no floors but were called balconies anyway. Fortunately the windows didn't open, so nobody tried to step out for a breath of air.

At the end of each corridor was the surveillance room where the security guards watched the nurses undress. Someone spread the rumour that the second camera was in the bidet and everyone stopped using it. Later a Department of Rumours was established to do the job properly. Occasionally a lucky fella would be invited to watch the monitoring screens; the price was a bottle of Dimple Haig or a crate for selected Saudi visitors, entertained at great expense by the Authorities in return for their support at interminable conferences on the merits of the home team's case in the war. More spent their time ogling the girls by the pool from the camouflage of their rooms.

Awake until dawn, England remembered their last time together. The night flight from Saudi where he knew, despite himself, that he had driven her into the American's

8

arms. Maybe she had opened the door, but he had already forgiven her in his heart. His anger was reserved for the other and his revenge would come at another time, or so he dreamed.

He'd arrived in the grey dawn at Heathrow, in good shape, for he had sacrificed drink in belated realisation that it was responsible for most of his problems. He remembered the cold, the frost as keen as his grief and her pale, sleepless face of beauty as she came uncertainly towards him. How could he not have cherished her? Then the awful, souless coffee shop where she had surprised him with the finality of her plan.

He had been stunned into silence at the futility of his own future and, above all, by her utter calm. He had been to the other side of darkness since her abrupt departure some weeks before but this was much, much worse.

Then the drive, first west, then north to his beloved Yorkshire Dales and Moors where, perhaps in pity, but certainly with charity she had saved his life. The confusion over room bookings at the conference centre, where he, God knows why had arranged to attend a management course. Finally she had lain on top of him, moulding her body to his in the final primaeval act of protection and wiped away his tears.

Then, for the first time in sixteen years of marriage, they had talked without bitterness of the pain and occasional laughter of two trapped people who could not live together or apart. For now he would do anything to win her back, overplayed his hand, could not leave her alone, bought her daffodils to symbolise his hopeless spring and tried to convince them both of his belated reform. Too late he had given her all his love and more.

South again, their two fine sons back in the calm care of the monks, an anchor in their early storm and so to final departure: she west to plunder their home, he east to the

Big City where sleek fat cats recruited mercenary doctors in large thickly-carpeted offices and sent them to the latest war. Whether against disease or fellow men, the recruitment fee was the same. So was the outcome.

2

It being Friday, England rose late the following day. The muzzein's recorded voice summoned the faithful to midday prayer as he set out from the hotel to the hospital, following vague directions from a hungover nurse who was herself meandering towards the pool. Here that unique cracking sound of opening Ferida bottles could already be heard as the weekly chess-by-the pool tournament began.

He passed the Ministry of Defence building, outside which a great rampart of concrete was rising, symbol to the Iraqi's obsessive fear of car bombs. Security, however, as with all Arab enterprises, was variable. One locum anaesthetist on his way to the hotel one dark night mistook the Ministry building for his accommodation and reached the fourth floor. Realising his mistake he left by the front door and waved to the guards. To their credit they waved back.

Despite the war the atmosphere was much more relaxed than Saudi, where there was a sinister background of oppression, none more so than on the occasional Friday around this time after midday prayers when the central car park was cleared and various murderers and the odd adulterer were relieved of their heads. England had rather admired their radical head and neck surgery but had been sickened by the ensuing applause.

Yes, he thought to himself, *much more relaxed here.*

The high-rise apartment blocks, between which he was

passing and into one of which the Irish later decamped, were filled with children's laughter and songs. Only once had he heard that in Saudi, down on the Yemen border. Saudis had no music he thought bitterly, in fact they never created anything; they would have missed the oil if it hadn't seeped through the ground.

Thus cheered by condemning a race he had come to dislike for their arrogance and intolerance, he had at last entered the hospital, Ibn-Al-Bitar, named after a famous Iraqi physician, the Irish hospital, Sodom's answer to the Harley Street Clinic or more precisely, the Black Rock Clinic. He had run into a temporary liquidity problem and had no dollars to send his people (or some of his chosen people) to Harley Street. So as he put it rather grandly one day on television, he had brought Harley Street to his people.

'God help 'em', England muttered to himself.

But perhaps they are lucky, Harley Street had an awesome reputation for ripping off Arabs, as he explained to the hospital guard in Dad's Army uniform and that he had just arrived etc, etc. After five minutes it dawned on him that this chap didn't speak English and he was about to do the trick of shouting at the natives, when an unfairly pretty Iraqi girl appeared at the front door.

'Hello doctor.'

'Well, hi.'

Cursing himself for his Americanization, he nevertheless put on his charming sincere face, as Adam burst through.

'I've just arrived, would you have time to show me around?'

'Of course, with much pleasure. I am Selwa, I translate for the patients.'

Keeping his thoughts to himself about pleasure, for his post-alcoholic randiness had now reached epic proportions, he tried to concentrate on the song rather than the singer.

The building was single storey, temporary, but high quality. The beds were full, although the place had only been opened a few months. What a contrast to the Americans, he thought sourly, who in his previous post had taken a year drawing up procedures for the hospital; not one patient had entered.

'Where do most of the patients come from?'

'All over Iraq, anyone can come here.'

She trailed off and blushed, as the party line emerged somewhat shakily from those beautiful lips. He grinned and after a moment's hesitation, she grinned back at him.

'My father is in security,' she said, by way of explanation.

He discovered later that most of the patients were high ranking Baath party members or "paying" patients, here by favour of Sodom's court.

They continued their tour. He noted the mortuary was closed, due to lack of spare parts. Junior doctors were urged by the matron in the same memo, "to bear this in mind".

He laughed out loud at this and Selwa came over to join him at the notice board. Standing close together they shared the vision of patients being asked to postpone their death until the spare parts arrived. Elsewhere however, there was an atmosphere of industry.

'I feel at home here,' he said to Selwa, 'the place is busy.'

'I'm very glad doctor, I hope you will be happy with us in Iraq.'

'Thank you. Do you eat lunch here?'

'Yes, would you like to come with me?'

Christ, he thought, *this is going to be awful. Party last night, pretty girl for lunch, what next?*

She was circumspect at first, over lunch, as there were other Iraqis around but the conversation eventually came

13

round to politics and medicine. He asked her what the local doctors had thought of the hospital.

'They were not pleased. It reflected badly on them, some of them are very proud of being graduates of the oldest medical school in the world, but they didn't speak out. The last Minister of Health did. He also mentioned the futility of the war. They shot him,' she said in a matter-of-fact voice.

'Pour encourager les autres,' he said, trying the sophisticated line.

'The President probably saw him as a threat to his regime. He failed to realise that doctors as a group are not very bright. They are not the intellectual threat that some people think. In fact, on the whole doctors are very dull people.'

'You haven't worked with the Irish yet!'

England decided enough was enough and thanking her, he was culture shocked enough to kiss her hands as he left the hospital.

What a bloody idiot, he thought to himself.

Still, she was extremely pretty. He eventually found his way back to the hotel where the pool was crowded. The standard of chess was plummeting from a very low starting level, as the players topped up from the night before.

God, he thought, *I'll never keep this up*, as he lay on the sunbed and pretended not to notice the figure of that girl from last night; lying a few feet from him, bikini top unfolded, but face down. Her back was gold and the gap at the top of those lovely, very long legs twitched to discourage the occasional fly.

He dozed in the hot sun and fleetingly felt her eyes upon him. For his part, he managed to catch the odd glimpse of white flesh as she shifted.

Disguising the bulge in his newly acquired trendy shorts with a towel (rather late at forty, but then so was the moisterizing cream which he had also recently started using) he retreated to his room for relief. He sat on the bidet and directed the stream at full power, soaping his hands. He watched in the mirror for a while and then closed his eyes to see the girl again. It was not long before his brief moment of ecstasy, the indescribable feeling of concentrated pleasure. He stood up; the bidet hit the ceiling.

Christ, he thought, *I hope the story about the camera isn't true.*

3

Winter came swiftly to Baghdad in the form of rain. Unfortunately there were few drains and the roads soon turned to lakes. Talk around the hospital was of boat building and water skiing. War came just as quickly when someone blew up the Central Bank. This did not affect the economy greatly, since there was no money of any value kept there, but for days afterwards dinars floated down the Tigres. Rumour was that the Kurds had planted a bomb in the central lift shaft. The Iranians claimed it was a missile. The British Embassy, the centre of the diplomatic universe, basking in a beautiful old colonial style building on the opposite side of the river, didn't know, but pretended it did in a series of briefings. The Iraqis said nothing but bulldozed away as much of the evidence as possible. Unfortunately for them, the building dominated the skyline and they could not disguise its mortal wounds.

War too, came swiftly to the hospital on the night of the pantomime. Ten dinars a crack for non-performers, the show was of the classical variety, sponsored by Ferida. Legitimate targets had been identified by junior members of staff for mockery. These included senior staff members, both nursing and medical, the management and anyone who took themselves seriously. The latter included the catering manager, who was one of those disconcerting fellas with eyes pointing in different directions beneath a dome of perfect white: the screaming skull and a real messer. In an effort to ingratiate himself with those in authority he had reduced portions to what the Irish, with short memories, considered subsistence levels. Worst of all, potatoes were getting scarce, boy.

Gentleman Johnny, the gasman, was in charge. Since he was almost stone deaf, there was no control over the proceedings. People fell off the stage; rehearsals were taking place at the same time as sketches. The Iraqis in the audience were totally bemused by the whole thing. It was a shame to take their money, but taken it was to pay for the magnificent surroundings of an enormous conference room, built for the non-aligned conference the year before. The conference was cancelled, it's difficult to be non-aligned and at war at the same time.

Laments had been sung, the juniors had had their fun at the expense of the director, who had been portrayed in a wheelchair pushed by the Matron. The oncologist had revealed an unsuspected talent for imitating walks. The end was at hand in the form of a heavenly scene involving the three surgeons, when the real Matron made a dramatic entrance and grabbed the microphone from the behaloed burly surgeon from Cork, O'Sliven.

'I'm afraid they've brought a busload of wounded to the hospital, I need some volunteers.'

The effect was of a sudden heavy shower of rain on a warm sunny day. The three surgeons, one in a nursing officer's frock, one dressed as a saint, the third as a virgin (much thought had gone into that) beat a hasty retreat to the back of the stage and headed for the hospital.

The double-decked hospital bus was a scene from hell as it loomed out of the darkness of the car park. Fifty stretchered men in the moonlight, some were already dead, some dying fast. The noise was of pain.

'These two to medical C. They've emptied the beds.'

17

'This one will have to go straight to theatre, otherwise he's had it.'

The two surgeons worked quickly. One fashioned a tracheostomy without preparation, for it was obvious the airway was smashed in by shrapnel.

Incision two fingers breadth above the chest bone, deepened in the mid line to the thyroid gland.

'He's not moving and he's blue.'

'I know.'

Forget about the bleeding, straight through the sinew of the windpipe.

'Suck here for Christ's sake!'

'Give me that tube, John.'

'In with the anaesthetist's tube, oxygen, oxygen.'

'He's pinking up, trying to breathe, fantastic. Let's clean him up properly and see what he needs doing. Relax all, we are in control.'

'I'll go and scrub whilst you take off those dressings.'

The filthy blood-stained dressings were soaked away carefully and lifted gently from the side of the neck.

'There's a large blood clot.'

'Leave it!' came the call from the scrub room, 'I'll remove it.'

The enormous jelly-like black mass was sucked away.

'Shit!, his carotid's gone, put your finger there and don't move! John, we need another drip and more blood.'

'Which carotid is it,' enquired O'Sliven in his deep, booming voice.

'There are branches off it, so it's external, so we can tie it off without paralysing him. That's the theory.'

Once again the atmosphere relaxed. The bleeding was controlled, the surgeons were back in charge.

'We'll leave the wound open. He is going to need skin cover and lining later, maybe even sling his colon up into his neck,' surmised O'Sliven, who loved surgery with a

18

passionate intensity. His bulging eyes sparkled with pleasure at the thought.

'Thus giving new meaning to the term, have you moved your bowels today?'

Laughter at last, some dutiful, they'd heard it before, some genuine. Relief, a young life saved.

'From the look of him he's Kurdish, probably shot by his own side. Word from the ward is that half of the poor buggers were shot in the back and you don't get that advancing on the enemy.'

John had in the meantime fallen asleep.

'Must be bad up there, lots of snow in the mountains this time of year. Apparently some of them have maggots.'

'Girls will love that.'

'Still, Matron will enjoy it, just like the old days, particularly if there is a power cut and she can dust off the lamp!'

'I didn't realise that she was that old.'

'But young enough to run the bloody hospital.'

O'Sliven did not like the Matron. He accused her of briefing the director each morning and giving him instructions for the day. He brooded on this problem from time to time and vowed revenge.

'Is there a bed in I.C.U. for this poor bastard?'

'Yes, someone just died, so we'll take him straight across.'

There followed the usual charade of lifting the patient, complete with several drips and artificial airway, from table to bed and across the corridor to intensive care.

'Hello Selwa, what are you doing here?'

'They called me to come in and help.'

She'd obviously been asleep but in the harsh artificial light that gives the patients no rest in such places, she was pale and beautiful. She smiled, they liked each other.

'So you have another poor Kurdish boy.'

'I'm not suppose to like Kurds, but I do and this one is pretty. I'll see if I can explain what's happened to him if he

19

comes round.'

'We'll have to sedate him if he starts fighting the machine.'

'I'll sit with him for a while.'

The surgeons returned to theatre and flopped around the rest room. Work continued through the night.

Two of the surgeons got watches from the Minister. England was not in receipt, but then he left early. The Minister, on a later occasion in the hospital, suggested the Irish and the Iraqis had a lot in common, they both having recently thrown off the yoke of Imperialism.

Next day word came down that the driver of the bus had made a mistake coming to the hospital, he just turned into the nearest one. The Ministry apologised, but it was also learnt that the other hospitals were overflowing with wounded, despite the television broadcasts of great victories and few casualties.

'Somebody ought to screw the bastard,' said O'Sliven the next day.

His audience assumed he was referring to Sodom. With O'Sliven you never knew, but as the President said each night on the television, all our planes returned safely to base, which is more than you could say for some of the nurses.

4

Salem, the Kurd, survived the night. Just. At three o'clock in the morning his tube blocked and had to be changed. By the time England got there, roused from his hotel bed with great difficulty by the switchboard, the nurses had changed it anyway. He generously told them that in future they could do it without informing him and trudged back through the roaming packs of dogs, past the Ministry of Defence (concrete higher) to the hotel.

He bumped into O'Sliven in intensive care at eight o'clock the following morning.

'He looks good.'

'Better than you.'

'Morning Selwa,' said England, ignoring the singsong Cork reference to his somewhat dishevelled appearance, smiling at the girl who was sitting by the bed holding the patient's hand, whilst he fought against the respirator.

'We'll see him after the meeting.'

'Okay.'

The consultant staff trooped in two by two, except the general physician, who nobody talked to save his wife, who talked too much. They sat in rows in front of the Director's desk, schoolboys in the headmaster's office.

The point of these meetings was never made clear to England who was more used to the cloying inefficient concensus management of the N.H.S. where, equally, no decisions were ever made but at least a facade of democracy was maintained. Here no minutes were taken. The rumour was that they were written before the meeting. The Director's view always prevailed, and appeared in the final approved version. Opposition was quelled by a loss of temper (signalled by a leaning back in the chair and the fixing of half closed eyes somewhere towards heaven as if invoking the Lord's wrath upon the dissenters). This tactic was reinforced by the knowledge that the Director was small in stature but large in influence in the small pond of Irish medicine where, like the Mafia, patronage is all pervading.

The rest of the medical Mafia council appeared from time to time, when they needed a winter holiday, or the Director needed a bridge partner. They were codenamed "Seagulls" for their habit of flying in, shitting on the resident staff and flying out again. The latter therefore became mushrooms and harboured great resentment, particularly since the Family had commissioned the hospital the previous year, whilst lying around the hotel pool. No one had told them that building had not yet started. This seemingly great achievement of accepting an invisible structure was somewhat marred by the fact that the eventual hospital contained mainly irrelevant equipment. Still that was a problem for the mushrooms.

In the meantime therefore, the Seagulls continued their paid winter migration, unlike Saga (the English holiday company, specialising in holidays for the elderly), where the client pays. It was fortunate there were no outbreaks of Legionnaire's Disease although there was a minor outbreak of a baser disorder, inflicted on seven male members of the staff by one young female Seagull during a ten-day visit. The question was asked: what happened on the other three nights? The Director was heard to remark over breakfast that she was a nice girl. He knew the family well.

The Director opened the meeting by introducing a

22

stranger to the staff. It was obvious he was not a doctor since he was wearing a new dark suit. It transpired he was from H.Q. His presence was unusual since his kind usually slipped in and out without seeing any of the staff in case they received an earful about pay and conditions. This particular morning, however, there was a message: "The Management would like you all to know how proud they are of your work in the last few months and how much your efforts are appreciated."

'How do they propose to show their appreciation?' asked Pete, the recently arrived Kiwi Kidney Man, with characteristic fiscal bluntness.

The Director eyed him suspiciously, perhaps realising that he had no effective weapon to use against this man.

Must find out who appointed him, he thought and continued to survey the ceiling.

'By involving this committee in future planning decisions and policy matters,' came the reply.

The Director was by this time very disconcerted and began baaing in his sheep-like voice.

'But there are no hospital policies,' threw in O'Sliven, who disliked the Director and consequently had lost two jobs at home already, since the Director was aware of his dislike.

Fortunately O'Sliven wanted back to Cork, where there was a different Family controlling such things.

'Does anyone have any comments at this stage?' asked Dark Suit.

The Swede, who had listened to the Management's inspiring and well-intentioned speech with rapt interest, intervened.

'I have not had a fresh Svedish Newspaper for seventeen days!'

There was a stunned silence, followed by suppressed laughter from the back row.

The man in the dark suit stared in disbelief, shook his head, rose and departed never to be seen again, until the Rebellion. The unsmiling Swede could not understand the scene at all and went back into his shell, a pale imitation of his Viking ancestors. O'Sliven decided to throw another thunderbolt.

'I understand there was a party, funded by the Company, to celebrate the sixth renal transplant. I wish to register my disapproval of these socially devisive events.'

The Director blew his stack, to avoid explaining the misuse of funds and there was another lengthy silence whilst everybody examined their shoes minutely, schoolboys reprimanded. Nobody supported O'Sliven who was livid and charged along the corridors to the canteen like a wounded bull.

A pall of smoke hung over the cafeteria. One hundred people were all talking at once over a hot drink called coffee, but almost certainly made from some other powder. The phone rang continuously, but nobody answered. The main topic of conversation was the events of the previous evening, for many a way of seeking information about their own behaviour. Rumours were started on their way, in the hope that they would be back by lunchtime with added details, the more outrageous the better. O'Sliven was holding court.

'None of you fockers supported me, the bastard got away with it. Are you mice or men?' and so on.

Dark hints were dropped about some of his colleagues' ancestry and connections with a certain potato famine. Such is the hopelessness of Irish politics.

'Now calm down, we have to go back to see the Kurd.' English conciliation which finally persuaded O'Sliven it was time to resume work.

They returned to the Son et Lumiere in the intensive care unit.

'How's he doing?'

'Okay, I think, he's managing on his own.'

England recognised the voice and those searching grey eyes from the pool. The legs were discreetly tucked beneath the desk where the girl from Mayo was filling in the continuous monitoring charts. He went over to see the Kurd who was by this time propped up on pillows.

'Can we take down the dressing and call Selwa to explain what's happened?'

'Oh, Selwa is it?' she said in what he thought might be a slightly sarcastic tone.

He looked at her sharply, but could not detect any guile in those grey eyes. She wondered to herself if his take-me-to-bed eyes would mean only for one night. Not that she was a virgin but, unlike some of her colleagues, she did not insist on adding to the Irish nurses', already glowing reputation for promiscuity. Perhaps it was the escape from the claustrophobic religious atmosphere of their upbringing. Almost overnight they had transformed the social scene of Baghdad. Expatriot construction men could not believe their luck and rushed to renew their contracts. Even the ugly girls had their fair share. Everybody was happy, but hoped the Iranians would not send a heat-seeking missile towards the hotel, particularly at night.

England examined the neck wound and pronounced himself satisfied with the appearance. O'Sliven, as usual, was stalking the patient, peering from the end of the bed then rushing up to touch various pieces of tubing, only to retreat when the clucking noises from the Sister became too loud to ignore.

Selwa arrived as usual breathlessly and explained to Salem the events of the night before and what would happen next. He grew agitated as he tried to speak but England, in one of his non-cynical moods, explained gently, that he would be okay and that they would look after him.

He was slightly suspicious when the patient seemed to understand, since English was not all that commonly understood amongst the Kurds. He asked Selwa to find out a little more about him.

He tried to engage the Mayo girl in conversation and for politeness sake, she answered civilly. Besides the question was easy.

'Are you going to the Villa tonight?'

'What else is there to do?'

What indeed, he thought.

The Villa lay by the Tigris across from the Presidential Palace, which was frequently and illegally photographed from its flat rooftop, together with the long magnificent sweep of the River towards the City centre and its Towering Twin Hotels, the Sheraton and Meridien. Twin financial disasters, they had both opened just as the war started. Businessmen don't stay where there's no business. One of these establishments had not only an outside space capsule elevator providing stunning views of Baghdad, but also one of those pretentious French restaurants with a large menu gastronomique. In times of war, however, you had to ask what was on, if anything.

That night after all the excitement of the weekend a quiet night would have been reasonable but, with their customary vigour, ignorance of normality and ever in search of crack, the Irish arrived in droves for one of the great events of the sporting calendar: the darts match between the two hospital teams. The Villa was dirty, hot and too small. It was heaving.

Later a large, beautiful, clean Villa was leased. Nobody went there.

The build up to this particular event had been intense. For days team news, insults and counter-insults had appeared on various notice boards, in such detail and with such precision that it was obviously a full-time job for the authors. Work in the laboratory and stores virtually came to a standstill. This was only marginally different from the normal state of affairs, since the manning levels had been set when all the tests were done by hand and now the machines had arrived (who cared as long as the Iraqis paid?).

Eight-thirty and the well-oiled teams had arrived, the official Company team in Lincoln Green, with Rocky as captain, unsmiling, for this was serious stuff; the opposition in T-shirts proclaiming that "Blacksmiths did it for fun". One of the young doctors was able to indulge his penchant for ladies clothing.

Blacksmiths had cheerleaders who immediately set up a cacophony of hysterical chanting. Ferida flowed down throats and onto the floor. There was an early punch up over the judging. The General Physician, as usual, passed out early despite his wife's incantations into his right ear. Surprise was expressed at his ability to sleep peacefully, since she was a blond lady of formidable proportions, possessed of a large lower jaw which when opened (and nobody could remember it closed) yielded a harsh Derry dirge. A voice which competed successfully even with Radio Baghdad at full blast. A voice for all seasons.

England having survived the display of national hatred, disguised as a protest against his judging (Jummie the Scot had intervened to avoid bloodshed) had retired to the bar and was accelerating into the Ferida.

Through the smoke and noise he saw the girl from Mayo sitting alone at the other end of the bar and, confident enough to start the hunt (which he always found more exciting than the kill) he approached somewhat warily, fearing rejection.

'Hi there, Mary isn't it?'

She hesitated just for a moment, as if contemplating retreat.

27

'Yes, how did you know?' slightly defensively.

'I asked Sister, besides there's a ninety per cent chance, if you're from Mayo.'

Yes, she thought, *you're the sort of clever English bastard who would know that, but what the hell?*

'So, may I join you?'

'Why not.' She shrugged and lapsed into silence.

I'll make the bastard work for it.

'So, it's a grand night.'

'Yes.'

He looked into her grey, cold eyes and hesitated, before taking the plunge.

'Look, I know you don't like the English, but I find you attractive and I'd like you to come out for dinner one night'.

He had raised as much sincerity as he could, for this important speech and she smiled in spite of herself.

'Okay, I'm sorry, it's in the blood.'

'Yes, I know, my wife was Irish.'

'You mean she's not Irish anymore!'

'No, she's not my wife anymore!'

Ice breaker.

'What would you like to drink?'

'Half a Guinness please.'

'It's off.'

'Okay, I'll have a Ferida.'

So they talked, mostly of other people, sometimes of places they had been and, in the manner of two people the world over when some chemical force attracts, the talk became more meaningful, more poetic, more outrageous, filled with a hopeless despair.

They were interrupted by a great shout from the dart-board. It was a shout for quiet. Jummie at his most solemn, a terrible sight which made a pallbearer seem positively ecstatic. Robin Hood and his merry men and women,

28

several of whom were by this time revealing rather more than Maid Marian would have approved of, were leading 4-3. The final doubles match. The gynaecologist complete with tutu was lining up the final double. Zimbabwean, he was known as the African.

'I hope his aim is better than this morning,' England whispered to Mary.

Leaning close to him, hand on his thigh to support herself.

'Why, what happened?'

'He had a sperm sample left over after the Infertility Clinic. All the patients had gone.'

'I hope to God the Iraqis don't find out.'

'I feel sorry for the poor sod who worked hard to produce a sample.'

'Is it hard work?' she asked, innocently.

He hesitated.

'It is where they have to do it.'

He was interrupted by a further roar. The African had made his double. Since he threw darts like a spear, this surprised everyone, including himself.

'I think they ought to mix all the sperm samples at the beginning of the clinic and add in a few European ones to improve the stock. It would also add a few live ones, as most of the poor chaps have only two or three to rub together in the first place.'

'But it only takes one, in the right place, at the right time,' they said together and laughed.

He held her hand and she looked him steadily in the eyes. He thought he detected a flicker of warmth, but she withdrew her hand.

'It's awfully smokey in here.'

'Yes I know,' he replied, puffing contentedly on his Davidoff, which the Minister of Agriculture had given him last week in exchange for the removal of a lump on his

29

neck. England thought he'd done rather well, but cynically wondered if the Cubans had visited recently.

Utter devastation was setting in by this time, as both teams celebrated the result. The young doctor, by now unfrocked, was attempting a somersault off the front steps.

There was an awful silence as he landed on his back on a car bonnet and lay quite still. Nobody moved.

'He's dead,' somebody whispered.

'No I'm not,' said the body and leapt to his feet amidst a throaty roar.

He didn't try it again, but the desperate drinking which only the Irish can sustain, continued.

'Would you like a lift back to the hotel?'

Transport was short so she accepted and they walked hand in hand, that wonderful gesture of intimate innocence, in the cool air of the river bank. He walked her to her room.

Fortunately her roommate was in so she did not have to make a decision. She would not have gone to his room. Not that night anyway.

5

Nine a.m. Theatre one. Salem lay on his back, his neck slightly extended. Drips to his arm and leg carried a slow infusion of fluid. They were supposed to start at 8.30 but England at the neck end had fallen in with the benevolent Irish attitude to time. No knife to skin until coffee had been drunk and views exchanged on Cork's failure to beat Tipperary. It was even worse if the mail came in.

The final factor was of course, Johnny. Johnny, as O'Sliven liked to put it, was in charge of passing gas that morning and there was therefore no prospect of the patient starting to go to sleep until Johnny had seen the whites of the surgeon's eyes.

Johnny gave anaesthestics according to his rules. Not only were these adaptable to any circumstances, but also multiple, for John would have none of this surgeon-in-charge nonsense; no mere technician's role for him, although that's what anaesthetists are. Like obstetricians, they've built an empire out of a naturally simple process. John's great weapon in this war was his deafness and he was able to establish superiority over surgeons by pretending not to hear them.

Salem finally appeared through the double doors.

'Looks a bit blue John,' said O'Sliven painting the body bright yellow with an early flourish.

'Looks yellow to me,' retorted Johnny.

Vince, John's minder, hastily switched on the oxygen without bothering the old man, as O'Sliven began stomping around impatiently whilst one of his assistants placed the towels to leave a large rectangular area below the ribs; an island of green between the yellows.

The Assistant, also Cork, was explaining that the Director had phoned him on the ward just now.

'He obviously wanted me to go and help in the clinic, he asked me what I was doing.'

'What did you say?'

'I said I was on my way to Theatre, then I asked him what he was doing.'

General laughter, a tacit acknowledgement that God had made a new mould for each man from Ireland's second city; no production line here.

'He rang me as well,' said the second assistant, bearded, Cork, best known for his rendition of a poignant story of Irish farewell involving a train. During this he would look to heaven as the sweet, gentle sound somehow found its way through a ragged jet-black beard and much local porter.

'He asked me about my trip. So I told him I'd been to Singapore, Philipines and finally Thighland. I told him they were all asking for him.'

O'Sliven, below the navel, had started without them and had already sliced through skin and muscle from rib to pelvis.

'Am I doing this focking operation by myself?' he said irritably and discipline was restored.

The idea was to bring up a piece of bowel with its blood supply through the chest and connect it to the mutilated upper end of Salem's gullet, bridging the gap in his neck. This idea had so entranced John that he'd gone for coffee. Vince was therefore in charge officially now. Vince never ate, but he did drink all night. His eyes this morning were the colour of bull's blood. He'd been celebrating his survival

of a recent highjacking attempt, whilst returning from Cyprus.

'I was sitting there minding my own business, gin and tonic in hand, when this guy next to me picks up his brief-case and takes out two very large hand guns. Next thing, he goes charging down the plane and shoots two guys who were moving towards the cockpit. At this point the plane goes into a dive. Everybody was screaming and shouting.'

'Weren't you scared Vince?' asked one of the girls anxiously.

'Only that they'd spill all my gin and tonic.'

'They must have spotted them at the airport,' interjected England, who thought he knew a thing or two about these matters.

'You could be right. Certainly when we arrived at Baghdad Sodom was there with the cameras, giving medals to the security guys.'

This of course was small beer for Vince who, like many of his fellow countrymen, had had to leave Ireland on the night boat to Liverpool in a hurry, some years before when he and a school friend had blown up the Women's Institute in County Tipperary with a home made bomb. He repeated the story now, at England's request.

'The building was on stilts, so we tied the bomb to one of them and ran off. After ten minutes nothing happened so we went home for tea. We decided to go back and have a look and, just as we got there, there was this bloody great bang and I can still see the ladies sliding down the floor in flowery hats clutching their bridge hands.'

He chuckled to himself and then concentrated on his job. He was good at that and never late, despite the fact he never slept.

Above the navel, Team Head and Neck were proceeding slowly since the scar tissue caused by the shrapnel had enmeshed the great vessels carrying blood to and from the neck. At last all was ready for O'Sliven to do his favourite bit, tunnelling through the chest with his great fist.

John had returned by this time and was complaining that this manoeuvre was not helping the patient's heart.

'It's not doing much for mine,' muttered O'Sliven and continued to thrust away until the great moment of feeling the English finger coming the other way.

Shaking hands in the chest was one of O'Sliven's favourite surgical moments.

The atmosphere relaxed as the tedious business of sewing the two ends together without a leak began. England left that to O'Sliven who was better, despite his shovel hands. They were discussing Vince's predecessor, a nubile Swedish girl whom John had pursued with great energy for several weeks, only to be pipped at the post by a male nurse.

'Any news of Olga?' he enquired.

'Still in shock,' came the reply from one of the Neck Assistants, whose drooping eyelids and laid-back manner, disguised a very sharp mind.

Laid back he had been, literally, one night when he fell off a high bar stool, glass in hand and bounced back up to the stool without spilling a drop, a distance of some three feet. A Seagull Neurologist, witnessing this performance wanted to write the case up in the medical journal. He'd never seen anything like.

Olga had been the assistant of John's colleague, a lugubrious Swede who survived only three weeks in Iraq. He had choked to death on a piece of meat in the hotel restaurant not twenty yards from two doctors who had failed to notice. He had fallen over at the airport on his arrival and banged his head on the marble floor. A subsequent brain scan showed no brain, but it was decided to let him work anyway.

The last few skin sutures were inserted, four hours or so after the incision.

'Did Selwa find out any more about this guy?' asked O'Sliven, stretching.

'Yes, apparently he's an agricultural engineer, speaks good English.

'They sent him down to Basra with a whole bunch of Kurds, they rounded up six months ago.'

'Presumably hoping they wouldn't cause too much trouble there.'

'Particularly if they're dead.'

'I think Selwa has developed a personal interest in this case.'

'I wish she'd take an interest in mine.'

England gave instructions to his other assistant, a tiny, firm female who had to stand on a box during the operation to see over the patient's head.

She was a somewhat enigmatic figure who used to give the boys dreams by confessing that her favourite hobby was sex of a particular variety. For the time being she was overseeing Salem's transfer back to intensive care. Her ambition was to work on an oil rig.

Selwa came to see Salem that evening. He was still sedated heavily, breathing with the machine's help. She thought how handsome he looked, despite his almost transparent skin and mop of dark hair hanging down over his left eye. She stooped to brush it aside, then glanced round guiltily to make sure no one was watching, for this was foolish. She had been attracted to this young man of an outcast part of Iraqi society, although her mother had told her there was Kurdish blood in her own family. Besides, this one was special. He was educated and had survived his previous ordeal with great humour. He quickly learnt the trick of closing the breathing hole in his neck so that he could speak.

She had seen him most evenings and in intensive care that meant there was very little of him she had not seen. It is not a dignified place. They had talked, or rather he had listened and occasionally commented as she found herself talking.

'Hello Selwa.'

She spun round to see the thoughtful eyes of the English surgeon looking at her.

'How's he doing?'

'Oh, it went pretty well, I think he'll end up in good shape.'

'He likes you very much.'

'And I like him and that makes it much easier to keep him in the picture. There are some patients with whom you really have difficulty remembering the only rule.'

'And what is that?'

'That each patient should be made to feel that they are the only one you are dealing with; that they have your full attention. I have to tell myself each time that that is the case, then they feel they're special. The problem is that some demand too much and put your back up.'

'Well that's not the case here. Salem is one of the least selfish men I've ever met, he's smiled through all that pain.'

'Yes, I know, I understand. But isn't it a little dangerous for you to show him so much attention?'

'Oh, I just say that I am the only Kurdish interpreter, which is true.'

'But he speaks good English.'

'I know that, but most people don't.'

'Any instructions, doctor?' came a voice from the desk in the centre of the room.

It was in darkness and neither of them had noticed the girl sitting there. Fortunately it was Mary, and she joined them at the foot of the bed.

'Any more noble thoughts on the conduct of medicine, doctor? No fine phrases, such as relieving their pain, preserving their dignity,' she said, teasing him gently.

36

He smiled as he remembered he'd been pontificating the night before. The problem was, he believed it.

'No,' he said, 'no noble thoughts tonight. As a matter of fact, standing between you two beautiful girls my thoughts are ignoble. Would you both care to join me in the fish tank?'

They both laughed at his reference to a single room round the corner from the other intensive care beds which was supposed to give some privacy as well as provide isolation but, being surrounded by a glass screen, was the focus of the ward.

He had compared this situation with the absurdity of hospital design back home, where millions had been spent on replacing Nightingale wards with small units. The designers then discovered the patients actually preferred the old ward, but they were asked too late. There is no privacy in a four-bed ward if something is happening to you.

They declined his invitation demurely and he was saddened that there was very little mixing between the Irish and the Iraqis, despite what the Minister had said. He went on.

'Have you seen Marwen today. I've been too busy.'

'Yes he's doing well but the parents want to discuss the operation with you.'

'Well, let's go.'

He kissed Mary's hand and brushed her neck with his lips. She pushed him away with mock severity.

Marwen was a two year old child who ran towards them as they entered the ward. England picked him up. He loved these Arab children, pity as usual, that they grew up. But then that applied to most races, he thought, as he played with the child whilst Selwa explained to the parents that the doctor was proposing a very big operation to cut out the narrowed segment of Marwen's gullet and replace it from below. She said it confidently, as she now thought that Salem's operation had been a success.

The parents were reluctant to give their consent, so they went through it again. Some of the ward nurses hovered around for they had spent six months building Marwen up for this procedure. Everyone was anxious, except the mother who had accidentally given the child the bleach which had burnt his throat. She was simply overwhelmed with guilt.

*   *   *

Six days later Salem was transferred to a side ward next to Marwen, who solemnly observed him from the door. Salem smiled at the child, although he was still drowsy and in pain. His doctors told him they had to "throw him out" because they needed the bed for one of a series of very large army patients, all of whom had tumours in their pituitary gland (or as England had put it, in the middle of their head). Seven had arrived in his clinic one day; all from the same regiment, all Goliaths.

Must have terrified the enemy, he thought, although like Goliath vulnerable to attack from the flank because their vision was disturbed by pressure from the tumour.

Anyway, Marwen was postponed one week whilst he and Jack the Lad, Seagull Neurosurgeon, removed the tumours through the nose. He had explained all this to Salem the previous evening, since he found the Kurd genuinely interested in everything. They conversed about Kurdistan and Salem explained his sympathy for the rebels, but not their methods. Nothing changes, English thought bitterly remembering Armagh.

He went to see Marwen and Salem the evening before the child's operation. O'Sliven was there arguing with the Ward Sister, a dried-up bigot. O'Sliven was giving it to her.

'I don't care what you say woman, the child has to have surgery sooner or later and now he's fit, he's on for tomorrow.'

Well, I disagree with it.'

'When you have a medical degree and take responsibility, you can disagree,' shouted O'Sliven, putting forward the old argument.

England intervened, although this particular Sister disliked him even more than she disliked everybody else, including herself.

'Has to be done Sister, Marwen is as good as we're going to get him.'

She turned away muttering and he shrugged his shoulders. O'Sliven winked at him and hummed off down the corridor looking for work. He was often to be seen stalking patients at midnight if his list was too short for his liking. There was a rumour he advertised in the local English newspaper, *The Baghdad Observer*, affectionately known by its initials B.O.

English patted Marwen on his curly black head as the little boy smiled up at him and then went in to see Salem. God, he thought, I hope we are doing the right thing.

Leaving Salem he passed Selwa in the corridor and winked at her. She blushed and slipped into the room, quietly closing the door behind her and pulling the screen across between the bed and the door. This is utter madness, she thought, as she embraced Salem and sat by the bed holding his hand.

'How are you this evening?'

'I'm better. As a matter of fact, I'm feeling . . . well you know.'

He looked away and she smiled. It was a subject not yet touched upon and she wondered whether to take the plunge as it was becoming of great interest to her.

'Have you had many girls?' she enquired at last.

He looked her steadily in the eyes and finally said, 'Well, you know, a few. It's difficult with our people, we live too close together, but at college it was easier.'

Again they were silent, following this confession.

'Does that matter?' he eventually enquired gently.

'No, of course not, I was just curious.'

He squeezed her hand and she leaned over to kiss him. She released her hand and slid it under the sheet and gently stroked him.

'After all this time, I won't last long.' he whispered.

'It doesn't matter, I want to do it for you.'

'Share it with me,' he said and pushed back the sheet, just as the jet of white fluid burst from him and struck the pillow behind his head.

At that moment the door opened. Selwa exploded to her feet and knocked the screen over onto the blue-clad figure. Salem covered up and moved his head across the pillow, in an effort to hide the stain.

Selwa picked up the screen and helped the Sister to her feet. They stared at each other for what to Selwa seemed like an eternity. She muttered an apology and fled the room. How much had she seen?

She raced down the corridor and nearly flattened England as she rounded a corner.

'What's wrong?' he said holding her by her arms.

'I was with Salem, in his room you know,' she trailed off breathlessly. 'Sister came in.'

He could feel her heart pounding as she searched his eyes for a sign of condemnation, but she saw only understanding.

'Did she see anything?'

'I don't know.'

He thought for a moment, then releasing her gently, he said: 'I'll go and make a few discreet enquiries.'

He never really knew; Sister was evasive.

God help them, he thought, *if she has a chance to vent her spite*.

He reassured Selwa, but convinced neither of them.

*   *   *

40

Marwen eventually made it to theatre the following week. England and O'Sliven were both tense. There was some shouting but the operation went very well. They both remarked on how little bleeding there was. Relaxed, off guard, final sutures, when suddenly the cardiac arrest alarm sounded.

The surgeons looked at each other aghast. They both had the thought at the same time and O'Sliven dived under the drapes. The drips had become disconnected. The heart had stopped due to lack of blood and neither had noticed. They looked at John, who shrugged his shoulders as they hurtled into the procedures for starting the heart again.

Nothing happened. Half an hour, the electrical tracing still flat, they retired to the coffee room. O'Sliven slumped in the chair.

'What the hell do I say to the parents?'

'He's my patient, I'll tell them.'

'No I talked them into it, I'll do it.'

'Tell them the operation went well, which is true because the poor little bastard didn't get any blood so there was no bleeding, but that we couldn't wake him up.'

O'Sliven was devastated by death. He blamed the anaesthetist, but knew they both should have spotted such a simple mistake. There was a shout from the theatre.

'He's going again.'

New hope for the surgeons. They ran back in. The trace was going without heart massage!

Marwen, the baby, who had spent half his life with them died the following day. The nurses wore that smug, "I told you so look," which didn't help.

He was buried next day, Anzac remembrance. England had been invited to the ceremony and decided to go. Perhaps a few beers at the Ambassador's house afterwards would ease the pain. He invited Mary.

41

Marwen was placed in the ground, wrapped only in a single sheet. The size of the rough wooden coffin had reduced the hospital staff to tears, for is there a sadder sight in this world? There was no ceremony, no flowers, but he was placed in a family area surrounded by a cage to keep out the dogs. The females keened and cried. Grief was for sharing and had to be shown.

At the British cemetery, all was quiet. A small band of Australians, New Zealanders and a few scattered Brits standing amongst the perfectly manicured graves of long dead Allied heroes, most of whom had died from Cholera.

The Ambassador made an impromptu speech. The priest had failed to show. He spoke in his gentle way of the meaning of Anzac Day and how Australia and New Zealand had become nations on that day when their young, naive men had been slaughtered on those faraway beaches. England pondered again the utter futility of it all, the waste and the indifference of the commanders, and here they were in a peaceful green oasis amongst the brown squalor of Baghdad, whilst the latest madman sent young men to die as easily as discarding litter. Which bloody earth were the weak supposed to inherit?

Tears came to his eyes as they stood in silence. The Turkish flag, ironically fluttered gently over the adjacent Embassy. Perhaps next year they'd invite them? An act of reconciliation. Mary noticed his tears and his embarrassment at not being able to hide them and held his hand. Marwen's eyes seemed to burn into his from the sun. So sad. So sad.

They moved off and the spell was broken. Pete the Kidney Man was already well into the Ambassador's bar stocks as they came to the real business of the day.

The hospital contingent was quality; Arthur was airing his views on the Minister of Health.

'When I was a boy, in New Zealand, flunkeys like that

would have called me sir,' adding that his father had been Prime Minister.

'No Arthur, he was only Deputy Prime Minister,' chipped in a statuesque beauty standing on his right; his wife, whose main task in life was to temper some of the more extravagant claims.

For Arthur had been a pilot, architect, politician and fruit farmer (Kiwi of course). Fortunately for him, he had credibility, he was an excellent transplant surgeon, Pete's technician.

He had also told the Director that his presence at a meeting would be inappropriate. The meeting had been called to discuss the recent bombings, each of which was getting closer and closer to the hospital. The girls were panicking particularly after Arthur, in his architect's role, had told them that the apartment block in which they all now lived, would come down "like a pack of cards".

Such remarks had built the legend of Arthur, already a folk hero with the Irish for his treatment of the Director.

Arthur was still talking.

'It's the first time in my life I've been fired.'

'No Arthur, you were fired in Saudi Arabia.'

He continued unabashed.

'I told that fella from Dublin that if he fired me for telling the Director to fuck off, then he'd have to start recruiting a whole new medical staff.'

This was in fact true. The Irish, sensing crack, had convened the previous night to discuss Arthur's dismissal. There was much talk of previous bombings concerning a certain post office. The Irish were on song, for they could intrigue rather than suffer. Bushmills was drunk, Carrolls were smoked and Arthur was interrogated sitting in the middle of a circle of doctors, astride a straight-backed chair. Satisfied with his version of the story, the boys decided to resign en bloc, that is, all except the Physician who was a

43

known coward, and the Swede who couldn't go home for tax reasons. The Physician was almost forgiven because of his home circumstances. Nobody forgave the Swede.

The following day Arthur was reinstated by the man from Dublin. The Director was furious, but had his revenge: when, later, Arthur applied to extend his contract the Director failed to respond.

Biggles from the British Embassy in full uniform, had joined them.

'What news of the car bombs?'

'They're missiles.'

'Yesterday you said they were car bombs.'

'We have new information.'

In other words, you don't know, England thought to himself.

He of course, had his own views on Embassy people. He was now giving Mary the benefit of these.

'The Foreign Service is a bag of nails now.'

'Why is that?' she asked dutifully, smiling.

'Well, the telex machine has replaced the Ambassador's job. Unfortunately, he still has to be there. He can't quell the natives now and tell the office about it six months later; he's now the boy who reads out the reply from King Charles Street.'

'What's that?'

'London, Foreign Office.'

'Oh.'

'The other problem is they rely on information from jerks like that.'

He pointed to Biggles and the small gathering of Embassy types who were about to make their departure and leave the backward Australians to their boozing.

'I went to one of their briefings about the bombings last week. Biggles had arranged lots of coloured pins for his map in the War Room. He'd somehow worked out that the Embassy was the real target and advised all those within three miles to evacuate.'

He went on to describe the Churchillian atmosphere with stiff upper lips. The Charge, a pompous bearded little man, whose way of disguising ignorance was to insert a long pause before replying to questions, made a good fist of convincing his audience of "British Business Leaders" that all was under control.

'It's all lies,' whispered England's companion, who knew a thing or two about bombs. 'They're car bombs. Some of the local boys having a go. The security boys will take a trawl through their blood in a few weeks. It'll all die down.'

'I hope we don't die down first.'

By now the party was in full swing, the morning's sadness forgotten. Arthur was explaining how he knew a bit about bomb disposal. Some of the Kiwis were performing a haka.

England talked to Mary. She had enjoyed the day they'd shared. He was beginning to enjoy her being around, holding her in bed, but had still not persuaded her to love him all the way.

I've only scratched the surface here, he thought as darkness fell, *although that's been pleasant.*

Marwen's mother cried all night and England promised himself he would not forget.

6

Finally Salem was going home, three months after his "bowel had moved". He'd tried to persuade Selwa to go with him, knowing the answer but desperately wanting to share his country with her, to make her understand. His only consolation was that he had to return to Baghdad for "tidying up" in a few weeks. Whereas before he probably would not have bothered to go back, now he would look forward to the return and the excitement of seeing his girl. The time apart is an eternity when you're in love.

England had been more successful. He discussed the problem with Salem, sitting on the end of the bed.

'So tomorrow you go to Kurdistan?'

'If only it was.'

'Well, maybe one day. I was there myself, just before your little accident.'

'That's unusual, most people won't go that far north. Some of my countrymen have a liking for foreigners.'

'You mean as guests?'

'Yes, the only problem is that they insist on these guests enjoying hospitality until someone pays the bill.'

'Oh, I see what you mean. As a matter of fact, one of our doctors very carelessly gave his vehicle away in your part of the world.'

'You mean as the Irish contribution to the Third World?'

'Well he was slightly influenced by the fact that the taxi driver who had forced him into the side was pointing a gun at him. He tried to get them to take his wife, but they took the car instead.'

'They like those four-wheel-drive Patrols. They take the top off and put a mounted sub-machine gun on the back.'

'Yes, I've seen them riding around like Spartacus.'

'Who?'

'He was a Roman slave who was good at driving chariots.'

'Oh.'

'I think he still has some followers in Saudi Arabia. I was once asked to see a young boy who'd been standing on the back of a Toyota truck when the driver managed to hit our perimeter fence. Presumably he'd been driving the usual way, that is, left arm dangling from the window with the loose Rolex watch and the other hand up his nose. Under the circumstances accidents are comparatively few. Anyway, at this point the boy shot over the top of the fence and landed inside the military hospital compound.'

'Was he Okay?'

'Oh yes, I think he landed on his head. I suggested to the Base Commander they arrest him for illegal entry!'

'Did he see the joke?'

'No.'

'Well, the Saudi's are not renowned for their sense of humour.'

'Nor for their humility, even though it's wrong to generalise on nations. I found them very difficult patients. They wanted curing yesterday. I once told the same Base Commander that his men were taking too many anti-biotics.'

'What did he say?'

'He threatened to lock me up if I wasn't available to treat his men the way they wanted.'

'What did you do?'

'I gave them what they wanted, including the Base Commander, whose main problem was seasickness, "Kiss me Ali." '

'Why was that a problem?'

'Because it was a navy base.'

Salem burst out laughing.

'But the Saudis don't have a navy, surely?'

'Well, they did have a problem of not having any ships at that time. The Americans had sold them the whole package, including lots of equipment they couldn't otherwise get rid off.'

'You mean, they cheated them?'

'Yes, the usual rip off. The Saudis at that time had so much money they were like children in a toy shop. The Americans simply helped them to spend it.'

'That's the problem with Arabs having so much sudden wealth. They can't cope. All they've done is to ape the Westerner with vulgar enthusiasm. They haven't invested the money, they've just learned how to spend it.'

He stood up and shook hands with Salem, who embarrassed him by kissing his hand and raised it to his forehead, the traditional gesture of obedience.

'Thank you for everything!'

'Go well, my friend, and stay out of trouble in Arbil!'

He passed Selwa on the way out of the hospital and told her not to tire the patient. She blushed, smiled and walked on knowing, as everyone else in the hospital knew, that the doctor was away south with his girl for the weekend. The poor fool hummed along the short dusty road to the apartment block where everybody now lived, fondly believing that his trip was secret. Some hope in a place where gossip was the elixir. The Irish idea of secrecy was to whisper.

*　　*　　*

Mary was late as usual and he fidgeted in the courtyard aware of eyes above the battlements; balcony walls that grew progressively higher as you headed to the sky.

Gentle John had once, inadvertently, ended up naked in the lift and had managed to walk the length of the balcony before he was spotted and escorted back to his apartment by two of his nurse minders.

This was one better than his previous escapade when, late one night on the way home from the Director's farewell party, he managed to get himself arrested by knocking on what he thought was his own apartment block door, waking the rather irate Arab residents and discovering that he'd got the right apartment but the wrong block. His white hair saved him.

So they headed south towards Babylon, for a short stumble around the piles of rubble, which the Iraqis claimed to have restored. At least the Processional Way was intact.

'Where are the Hanging Gardens?'

'I think it's that pile of rubble heading down to the river.'

'Let's go and have a look.'

The river was the best bit, a lovely reedy sweep with the new Babylon on the opposite bank.

'Must have been a fantastic place.'

'Difficult to imagine. Anyway, you've seen one ruin, you've seen them all.'

He was irritated because of her lateness and, as always, anxious to get on, as the way was long to Basra, their destination. She sensed his impatience and suggested they moved on.

Tea in Quorna, where the rivers meet. They stood hand in hand in front of the statue of the Goddess of Fertility and looked down at the joining of the waters. The Garden of Eden.

'The Iranians took this last year.'

'Really?'

'Yes but not for long, the Iraqis put up their gunships and mowed them down in their inflatables, young boys. The reeds couldn't protect them. Apparently the water was red.'

'This is where the Marsh Arabs start isn't it?'

'Yes, but I think it's where they finish as well. Sodom made them cut down all the reeds because he said they were providing cover. God knows what they'll do for building materials. Four thousand years wiped out in one week. Misfortunes of war.'

At that point the watchman came over and beckoned them to follow. He took them along the bank and showed them a log mounted ceremoniously on a plinth.

'What is it?'

'He says, it's Abraham's Tree.'

'That's a very modern looking rusty nail stuck in the end.'

'It requires a little imagination.'

They shared the delicious intimate moment which would stay in their hearts forever. She was happy with him and her previous doubts about the weekend began to evaporate.

'Look!' she cried and, letting go of his hand, she ran off towards the Tourist Hotel.

He followed more sedately, as befitted his age and nationality which forbade too much show of enthusiasm about anything and found her staring at a kiosk.

'It's closed!' she wailed.

Adam's ice cream stall, sure enough, in all its glory, in a war torn, small town in the Garden of Eden. Closed for the winter season.

They were comfortable with the silence which fell for most of the rest of the journey, particularly as it grew dark. United now in fear, they ran the gauntlet of tank transporters heading in the opposite direction, but on the same side of the road. Lights apparently were not allowed. The road was strewn with carcasses, animal, human and vehicular. A taxi with coffin aloft lay on its side with one wheel spinning slowly. They at last entered Basra. Black flags, symbol of death, were everywhere. Basra. Sandbagged and Shiite, it was a toss-up whether the population feared the one in Teheran more than the one in Baghdad. England drove carefully along the canals, past the still bustling Suq, to the waterfront Sheraton.

'Look at that lot.'

He pointed down the Shatt-Al-Arab; ships were lying four deep as far as the eye could see.

'See how they put the rusty ones on the outside to protect the good ones on the inside.'

'How long have they been there?'

'Since the war started.'

'It'll take years to clear that lot.'

'Great contract for the Koreans, thousands of them with acetylene torches. Make a fortune.'

'You're always on about Koreans.'

'Well I've never got over their dietary habits in Saudi.'

'I daren't ask.'

'Well, put it this way, one day there'd be lots of nice black puppies around the base lovingly fed by the Korean cooks, the next day they'd all be gone!'

'Oh stop.'

'The other story is that the Koreans got the contract from the Saudi Wild Life Park in the south, but they had to restock it twice, because they ate all the animals.'

'That's not true.'

By this time he'd gone round to her side of the car to open the door. It was something new for her to be shown courtesy and she liked it.

'The other thing is, of course, they say that if the Saudis go to war with Iran the Koreans will get the contract.'

She giggled, hand over mouth, in a gesture he loved, then turned to stare at the hotel.

'Good God!' she exclaimed. The hotel had certainly taken some serious hits and had a distinctly acnied appearance.

The under manager came bustling out, seeing their hesitation and reassured them all was quiet. For the moment, gloomily thought England. He wondered if he would not have been better off spending Friday in bed in his apartment. He then saw her long legs disappearing up the hotel steps and hurriedly revised his opinion.

'Powerful force,' he said aloud.

'Who sir, the Iranians?'

'No, I was thinking of something very different.'

He didn't wait to explain, but went into the hotel and found her at the reception desk choosing a room.

He took over, masterfully.

'I booked from Baghdad.'

'That was very thoughtful, love, we've actually doubled the number of customers.'

'Let's go and have an arrival drink in the bar whilst they take up the bags.'

He sensed she was trying to put off the moment of being alone with him, in a hotel room; big step for a Republican girl from Mayo.

There was something strange about the bar. It lay off the inevitable atrium with creepers dangling from the serried ranks of balconies, waiting for Tarzan to arrive.

'They've put the sandbags on the wrong side,' he stated flatly and grinned.

Sure enough the inside of the outer wall was sandbagged.

I suppose if the shell doesn't get you, the sandbags fall on your head and kill you anyway.'

The room was twin-bedded, much to his disgust, but

room service explained that the suites, i.e. double beds, were all closed until the tourist season.

He passed on the news.

'Oh well,' she shrugged, 'we'll just have to make the most of it.'

Her doubts were beginning to return as she showered and changed in the bathroom. This is not me, she thought, but she felt a rush of excitement as she soaped her long dark nipples, remembering how roused she was when he took them in his mouth. He'd, on occasion, brought her to the point of no return simply by kissing her.

Bastard, she thought tenderly, *he knows he can rouse me and I do believe he loves me, but . . . .*

She was roused from her daydreaming by a thumping on the door.

God, she thought, in panic, *am I the aperitif? I'm not ready for this.*

There was a corner table, nicely presented, awaiting them. There were few other diners, mainly young Kuwaitis, waiting for the casino (foreign exchange only) to open.

Spoiled brats, he thought, *here for the beer and whores.*

He shared his opinion.

'Well, what would you do in their position?'

'Probably the same. After all they and the Saudis are payrolling this lot.'

'Shall we have champagne?'

'Sure, if that's what you'd like.'

'What shall we do tomorrow?'

'We'll go and look at the marshes.'

The food was poor, but wine and brandy took the edge off their disappointment. They were at one, even the Irish problem failed to divide them.

'Who do these people think they are?'

By now he was full of insight, remembering the blood-stained tattered regimental flag which the young guardsmen had carried to the opening of the Hyde Park Memorial. He'd witnessed the ceremony by chance on his last leave. It was the gesture of defiance as they raised their battered standard which had moved him.

He described the scene to her, tears in his eyes.

'You're dreadfully soft,' she said, holding his hand between hers. 'It's just the way of life at home.'

'But can't they see, your brother and cousins, that they're just doing the dirty work for a bunch of thugs who know nothing else? Their whole life has been about death.'

'The whole world is the same, not just Ireland. Look at this place.'

'Yes, I wonder what old Salem is up to this weekend?'

'Is he in the Resistance?'

'No I don't think so, but he has an awful lot of relatives who are. He was telling me that his uncle's group managed to knock out an Iraqi tank last year. There was a great celebration, until the Army came the following day and lined up all the men they could find and shot them.'

'Just like the Brits,' she couldn't resist.

'Yes, but this is happening now, not two hundred years ago.'

'But what else have we got except old dreams?'

'You have the best educated people in Europe, unfortunately they're your only export.'

She changed the subject. Knowing there was no answer.

'Will you take me to Kurdistan, one weekend?'

'It depends how you behave this weekend,' he replied with mock severity. 'It's very difficult now. The Australians, who I stayed with, have gone. They're the people who taught Salem at the Agricultural College. He gives a very good impression of the guy who used to run the place. Ex-civil servant. I made the mistake of asking him, out of politeness, about growing wheat. He treated me to one hour of how you put a teeny piece of fertilizer with the seed er, at the right depth, er. Still they were very hospitable. When we arrived at their camp, there was a notice on the door saying "make yourself at home, have gone skiing". Unusual in an Arab country. Sure enough it was true.'

'And now they've gone?'

'Yes, Salem says the project will collapse without them. He liked them very much, despite their accent. He admired their dedication.'

'Poor Salem, he's in a hopeless position.'

'You mean with Selwa.'

'Yes, not only is it dangerous and foolish, but there's just no way.'

'I know it's sad when a love is not returned.'

'Oh it's not that she can't return it, they simply can't fulfull it.'

'He'd probably go off her after a couple of years.'

'Ah you're just cynical, from your own experience.'

'And you?'

She looked at him straight in the eyes and hesitated.

'Let's have a nightcap.'

The bar had closed early, but form demanded one for a lift, so the under manager re-opened it for them. Then to the third floor, hand in hand to the room. He let her in and stood with his back to the door whilst she stared out of the window, arms clasped around herself as if in self protection.

He moved toward her and took her in his arms, gently. They kissed softly at first, then more urgently as their tongues explored each others mouths. He kissed her neck and suggested they continue in bed. She went into the bathroom but left the door opened and he could see that most sensual of movements, a girl sliding and swaying out of her underwear.

The only light was white, but perfect to see the outline of

her face. He slid the straps of her nightdress from her shoulder and bent to kiss her long dark nipples, sensing as he did the gathering dew upon her other lips. She began to move against him; there was an urgency, a wanting which roused him as she moved on top of him.

'Come with me,' she implored, as he softly stroked her wonderfully soft skin, pressed her to him with each thrust. He heard her grunt softly and made to enter her. She quickly rolled off.

'I'm sorry,' she whispered, 'I just can't let you.'

'That's okay,' he said gently.

'I don't know what it is.'

He stroked her cheek softly. 'It's okay.'

'You know you rouse me like nobody has ever done, but . . .'

Then, she quietly told him of her boy in Mayo. He strained to hear and was surprised to find himself in sympathy. It explained her reluctance. This man had touched her soul deeply, first love of course, and he had a sudden rush of realisation that here was another kind of loving, not sexual, but all-embracing, almost a form of worship, tempering all future relationships. He thought he still loved her but in these moments of great clarity, which lying in bed with someone often brings, he realised the hopelessness of it all.

'What are you thinking?' she whispered.

'I knew you were going to ask that. It's impossible to answer, as always. I just enjoy being with you and ask no more of you; the sex isn't that important.'

'I enjoy it more than you.'

The words just came.

'My love is in soft Mayo rain, in wild fuchsia hedgerows, in being with you. I learnt a lot last year, not enough to see the world in a grain of sand, but I can see it in a flower, do you understand?'

56

'No, but I love listening to you.'

He could sense her slipping away and cradled her soft body as the sweet sounds of sleep serenaded her dreams.

What the hell do I do now? he thought. *This poor old heart won't stand much more.*

He remembered no more until she gave him pleasure in the half light, but it was only half a love. It's not the same when you cannot share the rebirth of the universe.

Next day he was quiet, introspective, as they sailed in the old flat-bottom boat between the islands with houses of reeds and black shiny water buffalo, untouched by time until this war. She sensed his disappointment.

'I'm sorry, I hurt you last night.'

'No, no, you can't give what you don't feel, I've been through all that before. Let's just enjoy the peace here; we may never pass this way again.'

She smiled and nestled her head against his shoulder, but they both knew the world had changed.

They drove back the following day still close. All was quiet until they crossed the last bridge before Baghdad and he hoped she wouldn't notice what he had just spotted. Too late.

'Don't look,' he said, but they were both drawn to the scene of three bodies dangling from the bridge.

'Deserters,' he said shortly. 'To discourage others. They must have done it twice.'

'That's barbaric,' whispered Mary, curiosity overcoming a lump in her throat.

'We did the same in 1914, same sort of war.'

'Same futility.'

And he could not disagree with that.

7

Arbil. Four thousand years of civilisation, birthplace of the mighty Saladin, who had finally prised the Christians away from Jerusalem. Now the Ayatollah wanted it back. Dominating the city, the Mound. Each generation had built on top of the last, the oldest continually-occupied place on Earth. No-go area for the Iraqi Army, breeding ground for the Peshmurga, home to Salem. He had escaped the squalor of the area through the generosity of his uncle, now hiding in some cave in the mountains.

The journey had been long and difficult as usual. His medical papers helped. They were continually harassed at checkpoints, particularly as they entered his land at Kirkurk, the vast complex of oil fields and refineries stolen by Baghdad in return for the insult of nominal independence, the Autonomous Region. Every kilometre along the road were the anti-aircraft guns manned by traitors. Well, their names were known and they would be dealt with later.

The travellers had fallen silent as they passed three monuments to Kurdish shame, designer prisons holding thousands of his people many of whom would never leave. Selwa had made him forget, now he gripped the armrest and wanted vengeance. His mother had cried at his frailty and scars but he held her hands and diverted her to her favourite place, the stove, on the pretence of hunger. He asked about his old friend, the museum keeper.

'The old fool wants to see you,' his mother said roughly.

He looked at her tenderly, knowing that, since his father had died, his mother and the old man had found some comfort with each other. She knew, he knew and fussed around with redoubled energy, to avoid discussion.

'And my uncle, what news?'

'I dare say Talal will have a message for you, many are in hiding. The army has been very active recently. I think your uncle has had a few successes but the army take away everybody they can find. I wonder if it's worth it.'

He finished his simple supper and kissing her softly, slipped out into the evening. Amidst the squalor of the Mound with its crude brick houses and filthy narrow streets, stood an exquisite building which housed a folk museum. Salem's favourite place on earth, the one he wanted to share with Selwa.

'Ya Talal!' he shouted and ran into the courtyard where his old friend was sitting in the last rays of the sun.

'Ya Salem, my boy.' The old man grasped him in his still muscular arms and kissed him tenderly on both cheeks.

'But you've lost a little weight.'

'I couldn't eat for months; even now it's difficult. But you would be the same, if your arse was in your chest.'

He then preceded to explain as the old man, who devoured anything new, listened his eyes sparkling, for he loved the boy.

'They looked after you well, those western doctors?'

'They were fantastic, good people. They are like us in many ways, the Irish that is, full of poetry and mystery.'

He looked around the familiar room.

'Let's go out onto the balcony.'

The old man smiled and led the way through the dark quiet rooms and opened the last door. They sat on the balcony, clinging precariously to the building, several hundred feet up the side of the Mound.

He watched with undisguised pleasure as the storks circled beneath him and landed awkwardly on their nest on the top of the minaret. The sun slipped quickly away to his right bathing the tops of the snow capped mountains to his left in a pink mist.

My land, he thought.

Below, the ceaseless activity of the Suq which continued despite the haunting call to prayer. His friend the Englishman had once told him that the shops closed in Saudi during prayer time. No one dared to defy the Religious Police there, as the doors opened and closed five times a day. At least it gave the shopkeepers some exercise, was the doctor's usual cynical comment, otherwise they would have sat all day.

'So what news from my uncle?'

'He wants to see you tomorrow, I will go with you.'

'Do the people still support him?'

'Oh yes, despite the hardship, or maybe because of it. They rounded up all our young boys last week, packed them off south, to die in the marshes.'

'I know, I was there. It was awful, but the Iranians were worse off, slaughtered lambs on the alter of one man's ego. On the promise of a place in Heaven, he sent his boys and some girls into our guns. I can still see them, red-head bands glowing, struggling up to their waists in mud, unable to move, as gunships mowed them down. They just kept on coming, but flesh against metal is an unequal contest. There were few left to catch the ebb tide home. Their hospital trains are old and weary. Many die in sight of home through lack of blood. Such a waste.'

The old man sighed. 'Well, it's only continuing something that's been going on and off for two thousand years. The only time it stopped was when Turkey ran the place, but at the price of destroying Arab thinking. It will go on because nobody who matters, wants it to end. Sodom doesn't care if we are wiped out.'

'Yes I thought about that. If it does end, he is in trouble but we're in bigger trouble. What is he going to do with half a million men with guns and no jobs? Because the women have taken them all.'

'In most cases, probably do them better, the ultimate blow to Arab pride.' he chuckled.

'I think he will send the army against us. Genocide. After all, his propaganda machine is excellent. He managed to convince everybody that, despite the fact that he sent his army across the Shatt, the Iranians started it.'

'It's a personal thing. He's piqued because he gave Khomeini sanctuary when the Shah kicked him out. You know he was in Kerbala for a long time.'

'Yes, Guardian of the Holy Mosque. It's ironic that the Shiite shrine should be here.'

'Well, at least someone is smiling and saying very little.'

'Who is that.'

'The Israelis of course. I hear they're supplying weapons to our enemies. That has to be the most unholy alliance of all times!'

'Practical people, the Jews.'

'Yes, divide the enemy. Not too difficult in the case of our people. How is it that one hundred and fifty million people can't defeat three?'

'Bad government, greed, wasted money. Above all because Arab unity is an impossible dream. Can you ever see Sodom and that other butcher in Syria ever agreeing on anything?'

'No, but I remember Hama. He wiped out a city because he thought there was opposition there; women, children, the lot.'

'Well, we are no better, look at what those animals in the PKK are doing in Turkey. Can you see us agreeing to govern Kurdistan with them?'

61

'Well, I don't know, but I do know I have to support my uncle, despite my reservations about nationalism which, after all, is simply saying that because of where you come from you are better than next door.'

'I heard it put a different way. The spirit that makes a part of our society, us, act as if it were the whole of society.'

'Well, that's too high for me. All I know is that despite the two thousand television war communiques saying we won, half a million are dead.'

They talked into the night which had come swiftly, for here there is no twilight. Salem was uneasy. The old man had hinted that his uncle had something for him to do in Baghdad. Sleep took him only at dawn. Another day of death in the cold mountains, on the desert plains and, far to the south, the blood-red sun rose over the still marshes. For many, there would be no sunset.

Salem lay awake on his mattress, thinking of his uncle's last comment. It's said the Vietnam war began to end the day coffins arrived in the small Mid-West towns, where patriotism is at its fiercest. Well here they've been arriving for two years in every town and village and that can't go on, particularly where the people live in fear. One day they will rise up from these same small villages and say: "no more".

8

Salem rose early the following morning, for the journey would be long and hard and it would be late afternoon before he reached his destination. The old man was already breakfasting and talking to his mother as he entered the kitchen.

The motorbike and side car turned off the road out of Arbil and bumped along the track winding upwards towards the snowcapped mountains. Talal had not told him exactly where they were going but he knew the last part would be on foot and wondered if, in his present weak state, he would be up to it. He looked at the old man, like some World War I pilot, tough arms wrestling with the handles. He had no fear of his stamina. Salem was glad in a way that the noise of the machine made conversation impossible as he had to clear his thoughts for this first meeting with his uncle for many months. What would they ask of him?

It was early afternoon when the track finally became impossible, even for the old man and they dismounted and pushed the machine behind a clump of rocks. They sat in silence for a few moments, savouring the surroundings. Above, the hawks hovered and dived out of the snow.

'Fantastic,' Salem said, breathing in the fresh mountain air.

Below they could see the soldiers on the outskirts of

Rayat checking all the vehicles.

'Bastards,' said the old man, with uncharacteristic venom.

'Well, I don't suppose they like being there any more than we want them. They'd prefer to be at home in the south. You can't blame them!'

'No, I suppose not.'

'My doctor told me that he drove along this road and they stopped at the edge of one town to take photographs. Apparently the guards came rushing over and told them, no no. It turned out that it was yes, yes provided they were in the picture themselves. They wanted an excuse to nestle up to the girls in the party.'

'You seem to have got to know your doctor well.'

'We talked.'

'Well, we'd better stop talking and get on our way.'

It was nearing sunset when they finally reached the place. Salem had the impression of being watched for the last hour, but then he was one of them. The cave was large, dry and warm. His uncle greeted him warmly, fixing his piercing blue eyes on him. He was tall with the inevitable beard. He spoke quietly as big men often do.

'So you have come to see us at last.'

'I'm sorry, I got delayed by a stray shell.'

'Ours or theirs?'

'Difficult to say, but it hurt!'

Soft laughter from the men sitting round cleaning their guns.

'And now I'm told you fart through your nose!'

'Has the advantage of not having to wait for the smell.'

Salem detected a change in tone as his uncle questioned him about the hospital and its staff. He grew increasingly uneasy as the questions became more detailed and he tried to change the direction.

'I hear you knocked out a tank last month.'

64

'Yes, but they took a terrible revenge. They dragged a lot of men into the streets and shot them. Unfortunately for them it was mainly the cowards who wouldn't join us, but they took some of our children as well, to try and force us down from here. It's hard for some of these young men.'

He gestured round the cave where the handsome faces had grown grim.

'They want revenge and you have the means to help them.'

'What do I have to do? I am willing.'

'Wait until you hear my proposal, you may not be so willing.'

Salem listened with growing dismay, as his uncle outlined the plan. It was simple, swift and terrible. He sat in stunned silence.

'I'm not sure I can do it. These people saved my life, they are my friends.'

His uncle looked understandingly at him, moved by his dilemma.

'I know, I know, but it is a sure way of striking at his heart. It's his hospital. Above all we need to attract the world's attention and for that, in these violent times, you have to do something pretty spectacular. We have to show his vulnerability, but I understand your anguish.'

No you don't, thought Salem, for he knew that if he carried this out, he would have to leave Iraq, probably for many years at least and that meant leaving Selwa.

He was left to ponder for the simple evening meal was now served and talk turned to other things. One of the group had news from Iran. He too had returned that afternoon, but with weapons donated by the Ayatollah. For each side funded the others' Kurds to stir up trouble. There was however, as always, a price.

Salem, caught in a hopeless situation, listened intently, if only to divert himself from the terrible decision he would

65

have to make. The young man was talking.

'Is it right to take weapons from these people, when they kill our own? Khalkhalli sent the Phantoms against one of our villages last week, then came himself to gloat. He sentenced forty-five to death. One family complained that a prisoner had lost three teeth and an eye. Khalkhalli ordered the same for the torturer. The family intervened before the eye was torn out, even so, their son was shot.'

The old man stirred from his place by the fire.

'Islamic justice. Swift, personally satisfying. Khomeini's father was killed by a government official. His mother took him to see the killers hanging and advised him to be at peace for the wolf had attained the fruits of his evil deeds.'

'Where does that leave Khomeini himself?'

'Who knows? Condemned hopefully, but still riding high on this earth. He took full advantage of the Iranian confusion, unable to cope with their wealth. Some of them think he is the Mahdi they've all been waiting for, the promised one. Anyway for us it makes no difference. Both sides will kill us when our usefulness runs out.'

Gloom settled over the cave. They stared into the fire. Salem's uncle clapped his hands to break the spell and issued orders for the morning.

Salem slept uneasily on the unaccustomed hardness of the ground.

He woke with a start from his terrible recurring dream in which a large aircraft disappeared over the horizon and exploded. The sun rose over the mountains as he sat spellbound at the view, each time was the first. His uncle joined him and placed his arm around his shoulder. Salem looked over his land.

'Yes uncle, I will do it, but with a heavy heart.'

'Before you go, I want you to see something.'

They walked down the narrow path to another cave, the women's cave. Salem stooped low into the darkness. His

66

eyes accustomed themselves to the gloom and he caught his breath. On the floor on blankets lay dozens of small bodies, mainly very still. Some moaned softly.

'What happened?' he whispered to his uncle, then he noticed the missing skin, the fallen hair.

'Gas,' he said, 'the bastards,' and choked on his tears and rose. 'Yes,' added his uncle, 'I did not want to influence you. This happened five days ago. The doctor says they will all die. So say goodbye to your cousins.'

Salem rose from the cave, blind with rage and wept. He remembered the bright beautiful little girls he played with all those years ago. His uncle came up softly behind him and held him.

'It's a heavy price we pay for freedom, isn't it? One day we will win, if only for them. No one who uses those dreadful weapons can win. We must make sure he falls. Allah will give us revenge and justice. Go to Baghdad, Salem, we must have peace!'

PART II
TODAY

1

Salem slid back the door of the Nissan Patrol with trembling hands and placed the bomb carefully under the back seat. It only just fitted, but then it was designed to bring down a nine storey block of apartments. He closed his eyes and pictured the scene, then flung himself on the floor as the Iraqi soldier ambled past. He could smell the cigarette.

He waited several minutes, praying the doctor would not return for his car, then used the shadows of the car park at the back of the hospital to return to his bed.

Tomorrow it would be all over. He would be discharged back to Kurdistan, others would take care of the detonation.

There were just two problems: he would have murdered not only the people who'd saved his life, but possibly Selwa as well. His love, his life. He knelt in prayer that she might join him across the mountains but his heart was so full it overflowed and covered his face in a sea of tears.

There was a third problem of which he was unaware, he'd been seen . . .

2

Salem woke with a start from the same terrifying dream, but this time it was a towering building, not an airliner which floated over his mountains and exploded on the far side lighting up the night sky and sending flashes of light deep into his brain. Who knows where? Was that the dream of the dying? He'd always regarded death as the sleep without waking and knew it would come soon enough in its own time. There was certainly no need or merit in seeking it out for himself.

He heard the wailing call to prayer from the little blue mosque on the bank of the river not 200 yards away. He prayed fervently that this evening's worshippers would escape the coming blast, for sunset had been fixed for the detonation of his bomb. His it was. Even though others had assembled it, others would detonate it, he had placed it. He'd given the information that sunset was the most likely time for the vehicle to be back at the apartment block. He hoped that his friend, the English doctor, might be else-where at that time as he was in the habit of playing squash in the cool of the evening.

Salem smiled grimly to himself as he recalled their dis-cussion on the doctor's increasing girth despite the exercise. He'd hinted it might be something to do with the replace-ment of fluid involved after the game; ten bottles of Ferida were not on most calorie-controlled diets, also the Mansour

Melia was not that far away. He ceased his prayer abruptly and threw himself face down on the bed, disgusted with his piety in the face of such a crime against humanity, covered his head and wept tears of shame and frustration. It was still not too late; he could tell Selwa or better still he could tell the English doctor, but then how could he face his uncle or the vision of those little girls choking in their own blood, blood-frothy spit, dying, grotesquely swollen and necks blistered as pain racked their pitiful small bodies. If only it could have been the Butcher himself who was to die, but that apparently was impossible. No, he couldn't tell, and besides he was afraid of the Butcher's dogs who would tear him slowly apart to betray his people. He had no doubt he would have given them names and they would kill him anyway.

He shook himself together and washed thoroughly so that he could pray properly. He faced Mecca and proceeded swiftly through the ritual which had been part of his life since he could remember. Afterwards he stayed kneeling, praying for the souls of his victims, hoping that Allah would find a place in some other heaven for the Christians.

*   *   *

A quarter of a mile away in residential block 34, England too had been dreaming in the stifling heat of his apartment bedroom. Mary was lying next to him, her long flawless back turned to him. England was half dreaming, half remembering their recent trip to the lakes and how on the Thursday evening after the two hour drive out of Baghdad first by road, then across the desert to the vast man-made Lake Thatha, they'd unpacked and then plunged into the lake – bliss, heaven, ecstasy.

They swam together through the still, warm water under a glittering starscape. Back on the shore the glow from the hundred or so barbecues picked out the tented village stretching along the beach, expats at play. The hospital party was, as usual, large requiring several Coaster buses and numerous Patrols, none of which had broken down despite Rocky's presence.

Rocky was the mechanic and captain of darts despite the absence of several fingers from his throwing hand. His management of his Indian boys was something to behold as he bellowed at them in pigeon Cork. One very small Indian had revolted once and knocked the mechanic over with one sensational blow, thus creating the somewhat cruel nickname. The ageing fleet continued to sail however, until he resigned in a huff at the company's refusal to employ one of his friends recruited in a Dublin bar one long leave night.

As soon as Rocky had gone the company hired his friend anyway.

Mary was on song as she dipped and dived in the clear moonlight. She undid her bikini top and held it triumphantly aloft. England closed on her and more in hope and expectation, took off his trendy swimming shorts. He stood on the soft sand, waist deep in the warm water and braced as she moved astride him, curling her legs around his thighs. They rocked gently until he could wait no longer and came deep within her. Too soon, but she leapt away laughing and splashing as he realised he no longer held his shorts. This was the least of his problems however, as he kissed her gently and asked why.

'Because I wanted you too much,' came the reply, as he stumbled ashore trying to hide his nakedness and crept through the shadows to the protection of the awning draped between two vehicles under which they were to sleep.

He watched the faces in the firelight and slowly drifted away, draped around Mary. Jummie was describing his recent trip to Jerusalem.

He woke suddenly, 'Christ it's hot.'

Mary stirred beside him and, smiling, stretched revealing more than was wise. That irresistible profile, smooth curves.

'It's because you turned off the air-conditioning, it dries you out.'

'I think the beer does that my love.'

'It also has other effects.'

'Supposing I didn't feel like it now, but was extremely randy last night?'

'I suppose yours is the moon and mine the sun then. Besides, if you remember, I took care of that.'

Mary nodded and knelt over him and took him in her mouth so that he could watch as she knew he liked to do. Her eyes were closed, he stroked her back and she moved aside his face whilst he kissed her other lips. Soon, too soon, he arched his hips and emptied on to her breast. She quickly slid round and lay heavily on top of him kissing him strongly, then rolled away falling onto the floor. He turned over and opened an eye.

'This is no good, you know.'

'I do know, but next week I'll be gone and you can find someone else who might be more cooperative.'

'I am not looking for someone else, more or less cooperative, I just want you.'

'I know, but I can't return your love in the same way.'

'Then why are you here?'

'Because I enjoy being with you and you make me feel good and safe.'

'Not as good as I could make you feel.'

'Not that again.'

'You let me at the lake; I was dreaming about it just now. It's coming back to me.'

'I'm going to shower before anything else comes back.'

'Oh, suit yourself.'

Mary showered quickly and departed quietly, giving the

same respect to the sleeping as to the dead. She was already five minutes late, but had no doubt that he would wander into the unit sooner or later, despite himself.

She was sure it was not the Irish bit which held her back, after all it was only three months since they had been together at a wedding in South Armagh. They'd travelled separately, she from Mayo, he from Baghdad via Belfast. He'd given a lift to our Albert, the administrator.

As she turned into the hospital she smiled as she remembered his description of the journey through Ulster with all its bitter hopeless memories. They'd reached Armagh city with comparatively little incident.

Searching for the Monaghan Road, Albert had a sudden call to stool. Armargh is not the best place to be looking for a Gents in an English-registered BMW. England decided the biggest hotel was the least dangerous, after all the Round Table met there, presumably minus Arthur, and waited with engine running on the double yellow line. Albert, buttocks clenched, hammered on the door of the hotel and was finally admitted after they observed him through the peephole. Nothing happened for what seemed like an age and England was about to rush the door when Albert emerged at a brisk trot and hurtled into the car which was already moving.

'What the hell happened?'

'I was sitting there, pants down, when two locals came in and started complaining about the stink. I left as soon as they'd gone.'

'Did you wipe your arse?'

'There was no paper, I had to use the bus ticket technique.'

Albert's sphincter lasted as far as the churchyard when he suffered a recurrence after reading the first gravestone which poetically described a local hero's death in action. He'd been buried just three days before.

The priest was a hard man, but the singing was soft and beautiful. Afterwards they'd thrown caution to the wind and joined the motorcade in its fifty-mile procession across South Armagh to Newry then to the South and the reception. There did not seem to be much call for five star hotels in South Armagh.

She'd lost the rest in a haze of Guinness and companionship. England had woken not knowing, briefly, which country he was in, let alone which town. Afterwards he remembered the bride's mother's hostility.

She entered the hospital. Perhaps he would come one day and find her in Mayo and sweep her away. Mayo, where her brother was buried, or what was left of him after the bomb which he'd carefully taken to the wilds of Donegal for priming had exploded leaving four young Irish patriots to die in the lonely mountains whilst the men who had sent them lived off the fat of the land at no risk to themselves in a life of precarious violence and no contribution to Irish nationalism whatsoever.

Mayo, beautiful bog, where every other shop is a pub including the corner frock shop; where the wild fuchsia brushes against the car and John with no teeth, who swallows a cigarette into his rubber lips whilst lighting it, sells chocolate which is best before '48 and has a copy of *If* in his bar. Mayo, where the main attraction is the Priest's Airport where, miles from anywhere and atop a bog, traffic jams occur on weekends and people still wave to planes. Still at least those self-satisfied bastards from Air Lingus had had to get off their arses and fly to the West in response to Ryan's challenge.

Selwa passed her in the corridor, eyes fixed on the floor. She did not return Mary's smile which was strange as they'd always got on well. Mary shrugged and then remembered Salem's discharge was today. She hoped England would wake in time to say goodbye, for she knew of the bond between them.

Once, in extremis, she accused him of preferring boys. To her fury he'd agreed, adding, 'For their company'.

Bastard, she thought, then smiled, *perhaps he'll come to Mayo.*

Selwa was preoccupied that morning, not only with Salem's impending departure but with the conversation her father had initiated on their drive into work from Baghdad's southern suburbs. They'd always got on well, she knew he loved her and they had a quiet relaxed relationship spiced with the shared sense of humour. She also had his legs, which was a nuisance. Not that Salem had minded.

'Selwa, I have to ask you about this Kurdish boy. My watchers tell me you've shown an unhealthy interest in his health. Now, you are old enough to make up your own mind, but unfortunately in my position I have to tell you that some of my more enthusiastic colleagues have an interest in his visitors. For example, your friend seems to be fond of yoghurt, they're always bringing him buckets of the stuff.'

'Oh, the Kurds are always eating yoghurt. It's a present for the staff. They have nothing else to give. Anyway father, he's leaving today and that's the end of it.'

She bit her lip as she said that and hoped he hadn't seen the tears in her eyes and that distant, forlorn, vulnerable look which always broke his heart. Of course he felt it, even while watching the road ahead.

He swept round the one way system by the archaeological museum (closed again) and into the car park at the back of the hospital where the watcher in him took over and he scanned the building and people quickly. She leaned across to kiss his cheek. He smiled at her and watched as she entered the side door which led to the surgical ward. He knew the layout well enough since the hospital was part of his responsibility and, only a few days ago, his keen young deputy had demonstrated how vulnerable the place was.

Damn the Kurds, what more do they want? Yoghurt eaters. Another so-called proud race, what the hell have they got to be proud of. Whatever it was, was a thousand years ago.

He recalled the English doctor expressing a similar opinion about the Greeks; great two thousand years ago and downhill ever since. What should he do about the Kurdish boy and Ibn Al Bitar? Better let him go as far away from Selwa as possible. Yes, he would overrule his deputy and allow the discharge to go through, after all there was nothing against him. Not that it would normally bother his colleagues. Yes, let him go back to his mountains, at least Selwa would not be able either to follow him nor blame her father for his death.

He had re-crossed the Tigres, past the palace's back entrance, and then to the security service headquarters building where he parked his car. As usual his heart fluttered a little as he entered the building. Every day there was the possibility of the flung-open door and the summons to the palace. Several of his friends had gone and not returned. A regime based on fear has to reinforce that fear from time to time until it falls. They all fall, though at what a price?

Let's hope the next one is no worse, he thought as he entered his modest office and took off his jacket and flung it on the chair.

He yelled for his gofer to bring him coffee, thick, dark and sweet taken hourly and tasting worse each year the war lasted. There was a soft knock on the door and his deputy entered and smiled a welcome. He liked the boy despite his known connection with the Tikrit mafia with whom the President had surrounded himself. Once, in an unguarded moment he'd asked the boy why the dual carriageway runs out just north of Tikrit and why the new hospital there is only one of eight completed recently to actually open. The President came from Tikrit.

'Good morning, Chief.'

'Morning Sadam, how was your leave?'

'Okay, family wedding up north.'

He stopped and looked questioningly at the older man who smiled. 'Lots of important people there.'

'Anybody we're supposed to keep and eye on?'

'That's why I accepted the invitation.'

'It's a pity we can't just go there for the enjoyment.'

'Oh, I managed that as well.'

'By the way, I've decided to let the Kurdish boy's discharge go through. There's nothing against him.'

The younger man was silent for a moment.

'There's a lot of pressure to reduce the numbers, you know.'

'Sadam, the boy has been in and out of hospital for six months, one trip north, we know, to see his mum. What evidence do we have he was up to something?'

'He's had lots of visitors.'

'Then pick up the visitors.'

'They include your daughter.'

'She was interpreter, that was all.'

Sadam looked at him steadily, nodded as if in sympathy, then left the room.

The Colonel stood and stared out of the window for some minutes. 'I'm going to have to be very careful here, keep cool and low as usual.'

He'd survived with that outlook longer than most, but his heart often skipped and fluttered at night, and he was drinking too much whisky.

*   *   *

Salem was still kneeling when he heard the door open and the familiar footsteps came towards him. He felt her hands on his shoulders and, reaching up, grasped them tenderly. He stood up and embraced Selwa so tightly she had to appeal to him to let go.

'My darling what is it? It's not forever. I'll find a way to come to you. My father has influence. There is work in Arbil for interpreters.'

'I know my love, but there are things you don't understand,' he trailed off, fearful of saying too much.

'You mean about your people, they might not accept me?'

'No, it's much more complicated than that.'

'You mean what the President might do to your people when the war is over?'

'My darling, that and other things, I can't tell you.'

She placed her hands on his shoulders and gazed into his eyes, his heart, his soul, he could not escape.

'What things Salem?'

He turned away unable to face her.

'Selwa you must go, I have to leave soon, I can't bear this parting any more. Just remember I will always love you wherever we are. What we have shared is not just for one springtime. For me it will last as long as my mountains in Kurdistan, as long as you see love in me.'

She came to him and placed her arms around his waist, burying her head in his back.

'Selwa, please.'

She released him and ran to the door as the tears engulfed her. He stared at her and closed his eyes, for he could not match her intensity.

'Please go, there is no more.'

3

England dreamed and dozed, tossed and turned for another hour, then eventually gave up the struggle and stumbled out of bed. As usual, an arm or a leg were in the way; design fault, like the appendix and sinuses.

He remembered under the shower that Salem was being discharged today and wanted to see him off, besides it was Thursday and he only had to last out until lunchtime before heading off to the security conference at the Embassy Social Club, probably for the last time as the snotty bastards were getting stroppy about the overwhelming number of hospital people drinking all their cheap beer and generally enjoying themselves. He suspected the main problem lay in their Irishness.

He meandered down the leafy lane between the apartment block and the hospital, light-headed and with a foul taste in his mouth. He needed fluid and calories, but first headed towards Salem's room. He found him sitting disconsolately on the bed surrounded by his few possessions.

'Hello, Salem.'

'Hello, Doctor.'

'Why so glum? You should be happy about going home.'

'Well, I'll miss everybody here . . . you and Selwa. Yes, especially her.'

'There'll be a way.'

'No I don't think so.'

'You seem very sure.'

Salem looked down and said in a low voice, 'I'm probably going to have to leave Iraq for a while.'

'Why?'

'I can't tell you exactly, but it is to do with my uncle's group.'

'But that's understandable, I'd do the same. After all, we both know what's going to happen when the war ends.'

Salem looked at him, his thoughts racing, but did not correct the misunderstanding. It was too late. England sensed a change in the air but, assuming a dead end, changed the subject.

'Anyway, there's the security conference this afternoon, then squash. Not much, but it's better than festering in the room.'

Salem spoke with renewed interest, 'What's the security conference?'

'Oh it's a cover name for the Thursday afternoon drinking session at the British Embassy. The poor darlings down there have to relax after a hard week of issuing visas, of which there are few; advising on trade, of which there is none since your lot have run out of money and gathering intelligence, which they can't do as they are not allowed to leave Baghdad. Still, I'm sure the British taxpayer would be delighted to know that their accommodation is excellent and all found.'

'I take it you don't have a very high opinion of diplomats.'

'They seem to have conveniently forgotten that we no longer rule the world, they cling on in the hope of a mention in the Queen's birthday honours list and a pension, pathetic really.'

'Where are you playing squash?' Salem asked innocently.

'Down at the Melia Manseur, by the Mosque.'

'What time are you playing?'

'Oh, not until it's cooled down a bit, around six. Usually getting dark so that I can jog down to loosen up a bit without all the kids pointing fingers.'

'Oh, so you don't take the car?'

'No, no, it's only five minutes away . . . provided the dogs don't get you.'

Salem seemed to brighten at this information, and rose to say farewell.

'You have my address in England?'

'Yes, of course.'

'Maybe one day.'

They embraced and England turned sharply on his heel and left the room.

As he passed the main entrance heading towards the outpatients, he noticed three young men in Kurdish costume being searched at the front door. The guard was busy dipping his dirty finger into the inevitable yoghurt bucket. Satisfied, he dismissed them with barely ill-concealed contempt and they passed swiftly to Salem's room.

'Ready to go?'

'Yes, I suppose so.'

'Let's just get the hell out of here. There's something going on which I don't like. It's a good job the guard didn't stick his finger too deep into the yoghurt last night.'

Salem nodded, the bomb had been delivered to him, sealed, in a yoghurt bucket. He thought they were taking a chance.

'We'll discuss the rest in the car.'

Salem said goodbye to the nurses, all of whom remembered later he seemed uneasy, subdued. His companions almost had to drag him away. Selwa was at the door, despite her vow not to be. She shook hands formally and felt the note pressed into her hand. He did not turn round as they walked up the sealed off road to the car park at the end. Along the road were a few largish houses occupied in former times by the British engineers of the Baghdad/ Istanbul railway, the Arab leg of the Orient Express. Maybe one day tourists would return again to the Garden of Eden.

The older member of the group climbed into the nondescript Japanese saloon car and took the wheel. Salem lay back in the passenger seat and closed his eyes. He was close to tears, whether of fear, sadness or pain, he wasn't sure, nor did it matter. The two young Kurds leaned through the window.

'Is the bomb planted?'

'Yes.'

'Good. Well done.'

Salem turned to him as if about to protest.

'There's no going back now, it would be suicide to try to retrieve it. These two will detonate it at sunset, that's all there is to it.'

'The car will be at the apartment block,' he indicated with his thumb, along the road to their right as they faced the hospital.

'What if it's not?'

The older man thought.

'Set it for half an hour anyway, then scarper, because all hell will be let loose and they will pick our people up first.

The security guard was watching them closely from the shade of his designer sentry box.

'Let's go.'

*   *   *

Selwa opened the note in the privacy of the examination room of the clinic where she was assigned to translate that morning.

"My darling, I am to leave Iraq tonight, perhaps forever. My love will always be there for you if you can

85

ever come to me. I will think of you every night, but especially tonight as I wait by the bridge over Prince Ali Gorge where the oak trees grow.

Happy journey.

Salem."

Oh Salem, why, what's happened?

England entered the room and, seeing her distress, held her arm in a gesture of understanding.

'So he's gone.'

'Yes.'

'Well, I'm afraid the show must go on, even though on days like this the lines will dry up like the old comedian and the patients will never understand that for us each day is a performance. Talking of patients, let's see the first one.'

He waited whilst the throng surrounded poor Selwa. Queueing was not a natural activity here.

Part of their insecurity, I suppose.

He wondered if Selwa knew why Salem was leaving Iraq. He was roused from his daydreaming by a familiar voice.

'Excuse me doctor.' The belly had appeared several seconds before the voice.

England shaded his eyes against the tie and shirt of the Iraqi liaison doctor, all of whom had now eased into his room.

He had once recommended his tailor to one of the young Irish hopefuls who duly selected a nice pinstripe and had been rewarded with a perfectly fitting suit a few days later as promised. The only problem was, the stripes were horizontal. Had he been English he would have kicked up a great fuss. Being Irish he wore the suit anyway.

Still, Dr Baghdaddi was a nice man, just terrified out of his wits if word came from the Palace. Big Daddy spoke.

'You must go at once with this man,' indicating a tall unsmiling soldier standing behind him.

86

'I've got a clinic full of patients.'

'They'll have to wait. You've got to go and see a very, very important patient elsewhere.'

England sensed major problems: firstly, he had no jacket; secondly, he had a curry stain on his sleeve from the previous night and, thirdly, he had the serious problem of Salem's departure. What the hell was going on?

He obviously had no choice, and rose slowly from his chair. He asked Selwa to explain that he had been called away to an emergency, the perennial medical explanation for a doctor's absence, particularly on the golf course.

She whispered urgently to him as he passed. 'Is it to do with Salem?'

'No,' he hesitated. 'At least, I don't think so.'

Two minutes later, England was hurtling across Baghdad in a military ambulance, outriders front and back.

The convoy screeched into the back entrance of the palace and he was directed to a rather plain, if not ugly, two-storey building. It looked fairly new to his somewhat uneasy mind.

He noted the parked vehicles, all of which were large black Mercedes with tinted windows. It was with these that the Baath party hierarchy demonstrated their solidarity with the people. Indeed, there was little else since the party had been founded by three eccentric schoolmasters in Damascus with the vague platform of pan-Arab socialism and nothing concrete in the way of fairly governing a people. Besides, they were now ruled by the book according to Sodom, whose portrait was everywhere, lest they forget.

Since he was about to enter the Butcher's shop, England decided to concentrate his mind on the task ahead. He was shown politely, but firmly down a long corridor into a large room fitted out as a clinic. He sat on a revolving stool and swung slowly around, catching his breath. He rolled his sleeves up neatly to hide the curry stain.

Ten minutes later, the First Lady appeared with the Minister of Health (new, trembling and uniformed) together with several senior Iraqi doctors whom England knew.

He reflected on the way back on the inequality of the situation, whereby an important lady who had been dizzy for two days (he told her exactly when to take the tablets) took such precedence over those poor bastards waiting patiently for him in the clinic, mostly with cancer, some in pain, some dying. Again, he wondered which bloody earth the meek were supposed to inherit. Still, at least they hadn't asked him about Salem, and the First Lady was a nice one.

They worked slowly through the waiting throng. He skipped coffee as that would definitely had made him late for the security conference. Pete, the kidney, was on the phone several times to remind him of his obligation to be ready on time as he was driving the selected few the short distance to the Embassy.

One of his favourite patients, a young girl from Basra, had to be admitted, dying, after her twelve hour night journey by train. He'd spent time with the father, a small, shy teacher who accepted the inevitable with quiet dignity. England shared his hidden grief and thought of the terrible, sad journey home with the body. Another failure, and he couldn't blame Sodom or his wife.

4

By mid-morning the ageing Toyota had reached the out-skirts of Takrit. The air-conditioning had long since given up the ghost due to lack of Freon and they baked as the hostile Republican guard had them empty the car just for the hell of it, while he waved through all the non Kurds.

Salem was for saying something but the older man mut-tered that he should save his breath for purer air.

Eventually, they were allowed to proceed. Progress was slow as the road was narrow and totally occupied by a con-tinual stream of oil tankers with which Sodom tried to off-set the effects of the pipeline cut off by the Syrians. Salem brooded and came to the conclusion that once again the only sufferers from the dropping oil revenue were the poor. There seemed to be no limit to the amount spent on guns and warplanes as the West desperately tried to stem the Muslim hordes from Iran. God, he felt, what a man to choose as the lesser of two evils. He was sure that someone would pay the price one day for arming a madman to the teeth.

'Do you think he's mad?'

'Who'

'Sodom.'

'Mad? No, psychopathic, certainly. I suppose that's a form of mania. He obviously enjoys killing people and has to continue now he's started. But mad, I don't think so.'

'How're we going to get rid of him?'

'Wish I knew, he's so well guarded by people who know they have to keep him alive or go down with him, it's a great incentive.'

'Well, I don't think our gesture will make much difference.'

'Too late now, anyway. But you may be wrong. It may just show the world what a bastard he is and our own people that he is vulnerable.'

'They know that already, they just don't care. And more importantly they prefer him to Khomeini, at least the Americans do.'

'Oh sure, the Americans always act in their own best interest. They insist on sharing their civilization with the rest of the world. But they don't have any. Their idea of civilization is to create a little America wherever they go, so they don't have to mix with the locals. But the real symbol of American civilization is the golden arches.'

'What's that?'

'Macdonalds.'

Salem smiled, despite his black mood.

'What are the arrangements for tonight?'

'You cross over after dark. One of your uncle's men will take you. From there it's up to our Iranian brothers.'

'You think I can get to Europe from there?'

The other man looked at him quizically. 'Why would you want to go there?'

'Well, there's nothing for me in Iran. There might be something I can do for the cause in London or Switzerland.

'We've got enough hangers-on there as it is.'

'But I can't see me settling in Iran. In many ways it's worse there than it is here.'

They were proceeding through the outskirts of Kirkuk, the centre of the Kurdish oil fields, astride a muddy river and circled by missiles. Undamaged, despite mighty efforts by the Iranians to flatten it.

'What time in Arbil?'

'Oh, I would think around four. You have an hour to get your things together and say your goodbyes.'

'Yes, that's not going to be easy. My mother has had enough of seeing so little of me.'

'You have no choice. Once the bomb goes off they'll put two and two together and they will be in Arbil quicker than shit off a shovel.'

'So that's it then.'

'I'm afraid so.'

Salem drifted in and out of sleep for the next two hours as they sped north towards Arbil, once they had turned off the Mosul Road and left the Oil convoys behind. Mosul, the Christian centre of Iraq, with its many orthodox churches and the singing he always enjoyed. He mused on the irony of the freedom of worship for these people and remembered the talks he had witnessed between his uncle and the Christian leaders united against the common enemy. What would Saladin make of that? He certainly would not have approved of Sodom's claim to be a direct descendant, but then neither would Mohammed.

He awoke with a start, just as Selwa appeared in his dream nailed to a cross and receding even further from his outstretched arms.

'What's going on now?'

'Another checkpoint.'

'Don't these bastards ever give up?'.

'No, but if they do we'll have 'em. In any case this is your town.'

'But when will I see it again?'

The older man made no reply as they ground up the Mound to Salem's home.

91

5

'How many more Selwa?'

'Only one, Doctor.'

England was fading rapidly; he needed a cold Carlsberg badly. That first searing, almost painful rush at the back of the throat, the oral orgasm, particularly on an empty stomach when the alcohol is hoovered directly into the blood stream, then you are gone.

Must have something to eat before I go, he thought. *I wonder what's for lunch? Probably the Screaming Skull's speciality of chicken kiev with a choice of that or chicken kiev:* a particularly foul dish by which a completely tasteless meat (or fish-tasting because the chickens were often fed on fish meal) could be disguised with a strong sauce which somehow became trapped between the skin and meat and which gushed out all over your shirt when the pressure was relieved by stabbing the victim with a fork. Still, it's better than the beef in Saudi Arabia which tasted of cardboard because that was largely what the cows ate.

The last patient came and went. He wrote the notes and headed for the dining room. Tony, the laundry was already marking a new set of nurses who had arrived that morning. As each entered the dining room they were given marks out of ten like a diving competition, complete with cards held up. The matron was not amused, but then she was the only one with a minus score.

He collected his chicken kiev and found and joined the rugby crowd who stuck together even during the off season. That was just about the whole year, since there was only four teams in the country and, after four games against each other matches became somewhat monotonous, like Scottish football.

England was telling them about rugby in Saudi Arabia which was much more difficult to organise as the Saudis had twigged that rugby and drinking went together, so codes were used to indicate the after-match venue and tins of malt were the main prize in the draw. There was also the problem that the Saudis kept moving the pitch. One week he'd turned up and found half of a new Mosque on the site of the previous week's match. The best thing was the away fixtures in the more civilized parts of the Arab world. The conversation switched sports.

'We should never have lost that cricket match to those Embassy bastards.'

'It was quite simple, their Pakistanis are better than our Indians.'

'Then we'll make up for it this afternoon and try and drink them dry.'

Pete, the kidney, by this time was getting agitated so they headed out to the car park and drove the half mile or so to the Embassy compound.

The weekly ritual was repeated. Three heavily armed Iraqi soldiers had a list of names attached to a clipboard. If your name wasn't on the list, which was usually the case with the Irish, you simply used someone else's name on the basis that if they did turn up they could always do the same. It paid to arrive early.

They parked the Patrol at the bottom of the drive and strode past the cricket pitch and tennis courts to the river-side bar, which lacked only one essential item, air-conditioning. Instead, in true empire fashion, they had fans which whirled and drove the cigarette smoke down onto the drinkers so that by the end of the afternoon everyone's perfume was by Benson and Hedges.

England sighed as he entered and realised that when Mary collected him at the end of her shift, this would be her first comment. Still, by then he would be past caring. He'd promised to take her shopping as her time in Baghdad was drawing to a close and any case it would save him driving home and risking an accident, not that they had breathalyzers and they didn't lock you up like the Saudis.

They settled for a couple of tables by the dart board and the session began. Several hours of stories, comments, darts and outrage; women by invitation only. Real ballroom of romance stuff now confined to civilized areas like Ireland, Scotland, Wales and Yorkshire. England liked to think he straddled the two worlds but, unfortunately, in his view women and serious drinking simply did not mix.

Bernie of security and boxing fame, and the only decent one from the empire side, came over to join them.

'You boys heard anything about a bomb scare?'

'Where. . . . here or Belfast?'

'Here, you idiot!'

'No, there's nothing going on at the hospital, at least not when we left.'

'Well, they've been looking at all the cars at the end of the drive.'

'Probably looking for something to nick.'

'Well, mine's back at the apartment block,' slurred England. 'It'll be here in about half-an-hour. However, they'll have got fed up by then.'

'No, I don't think so, it seems fairly serious.'

6

Selwa was free to go at the end of the clinic, but lingered a while and decided to go back to Salem's room in a forlorn attempt to keep him a little longer. The bed had been made up, but the room had not been reoccupied and she sat on the edge. The door burst open and the small grey haired Sister shuffled into the room. As usual, her pinched face resembled a cat's arse.

'What're you doing here?'

'I . . . I came to make sure that Salem had not left anything behind.'

'Well, as you see he hasn't, so you needn't clutter the place up. Have you no home to go to?'

The insensitivity burst Selwa's dam of misery. 'You callous old bitch, how ever did you become a nurse!'

'That does it. You and I are going to see Security. No one insults me, and there's something they ought to know about your precious Salem!'

Selwa stood and stared at her. 'What do you mean?'

The Sister smiled. 'The only way you'll find out is to come with me.'

They walked in silence to the outpatients courtyard, now empty. The security office door was closed, but there were voices from within. Sister knocked on the door. Selwa was somewhat surprised at the warmth of the greeting for her by the normally sullen Security Chief.

'Why, Sister, how nice to see you. How can I help?'

Surely he's not doing it with her, thought Selwa wildly, that being the only possible explanation for such a bizarre greeting. *If so, they deserve each other, but stranger liaisons have happened with others, since the Irish arrived.*

'This woman has been extremely rude to me, and there's something else.'

'Let's deal with the something else.'

'Her boyfriend, the Kurd, who left the hospital this morning. I saw him in the car park last night. He was up to something.'

'What?'

'I don't know, but he shouldn't have been there anyway.'

'I agree, but what exactly was he doing.'

'He was walking, running back into the hospital from one of the cars.'

'Which one?'

'I don't know, there were about half a dozen in the car park.'

Selwa was silent, her heart racing. What the hell was Salem up to? Then she remembered the note. Security turned to her.

'What do you know about this Selwa?'

'Nothing, nothing at all. I said goodbye to him this morning and that's all I know. This nurse never liked him, I could tell.'

'And you liked him too much, and now your sins have been found out.'

'Ladies, please. Sister, could you wait outside, I need to talk to Selwa. Better still, go back to the ward and I'll see you later.'

The small figure glowering with self-righteousness gave Selwa a triumphant look and left the room.

'What's this all about, Selwa?'

'We had a row, that's all. She's trying to cause trouble.

We've never got on.'

'But what was the Kurd doing?' he persisted more impatiently.

'I don't know, he was probably just going for a walk.'

'Well, I can't take a chance, I'll have to call your father's office.' He picked up the phone and dialled.

Selwa heard her father's voice at the other end. She listened whilst the story was told. The telephone was handed to her. Her father sounded cold.

'What's going on Selwa?'

'Nothing Daddy, I've told you about this Sister before. She hates me.'

'I've got a bad feeling about this. We'll have to search the vehicles. Put Ali back on.'

Selwa sat numbed as she realised that there was something going on. Why else would Salem have to leave Iraq tonight? Suddenly she realised the possibilities and the implications for her and her father.

'You're to stay here, your father will send someone for you.'

He then picked up the phone again, and with a sinking heart Selwa recognised her father's superior's voice. Selwa nodded, cold, very afraid.

The door closed and she heard the key turn in the lock. *Damn that Sister.*

She looked at her watch, 3.15. Where was Salem? Safely in Kurdistan? She lay on the couch and took refuge in sleep, alone and helpless. What would happen to her father?

A catnap later, she awoke to the sound of the key in the door. Her father's deputy beckoned her coldly to follow him. He said nothing, nothing at all as they drove away from the hospital towards her father's office.

'Is my father still in his office?'

The young man looked steadily at her, but made no reply. Her fear increased steadily as they turned into the

97

car park behind the security headquarters.

Still without a word, he ushered her along the first floor corridor into her father's office. She recognised the figure seated in his chair and collapsed onto the facing chair, before her knees betrayed her.

The President's step-brother looked up at her and looked her up and down, unsmiling dark eyes, full of menace. His voice was soft.

'Your father's moved elsewhere and kindly loaned me his office for the time being, whilst we find out a little more about this Kurd of yours.'

'He was not mine, I only translated. . .'

He cut her off with an abrupt gesture of his left hand. 'Have you arranged to see him again?'

'You know that is impossible.'

She had recovered a little, and decided defiance was the best form of defence. Besides the statement had a merit of truth which gave her extra confidence.

'But he must have told you of his plans.'

She shrugged. 'As far as I know, he was going home.'

He was not satisfied. 'Selwa, we have to be sure, and quickly. I do not want to hurt you, or your father, but there must be more.'

She was left alone for what seemed an eternity. At least she was still clothed and had a watch. She knew how they broke people, but that was over a few days, and she knew also that they wanted more, quickly. She looked for the hundreth time at her watch, 4.30. Salem must be in Arbil by now, saying his goodbyes. Perhaps she could stall them long enough for him to reach Iran.

The key turned in the lock. The President's step-brother came in accompanied by two younger men in the plain olive green uniform of the President's guard.

'Unless you tell us where your boyfriend is going, I have told these two they can do what they like with you and, frankly, it is unlikely you will survive.'

'But I don't know any more.'

'Very well, but before you go downstairs though, I want you to see this.'

He unfolded a white sheet of paper. She stood up and looked over the table at the document. It was a Presidential Order, a death warrant. Sentence to be carried out immediately. There was no name.

'I have several of these. Your father's name will be filled in here in the next half hour. Now go and enjoy yourself with these two. When you are ready to talk and save your father's life, they will send for me.'

She was unable to walk from the office, so they carried her between them to the basement. The larger of the two, the one with the long scar running from the corner of his mouth, moistened his lips.

'I'm looking forward to this.'

His companion nodded and smiled. 'Yes, it's time we got our own back on that supercilious father of hers, he's been riding me ever since that Kurd died last year.'

Selwa was very unceremoniously dumped on a mattress, the only furnishing in the room. She decided resistance was useless.

'Well, we may as well enjoy her while she is still warm.'

Selwa opened her eyes and met those of her father pressed against the one small window in the door. His face was bruised. He tried to shake his head, but he was unable to move. She knew she had to choose.

'Stop!' she screamed. 'There's a note in my bag, it's from him. It mentioned where he was going.'

'Shit,' said the scarred one, 'I'll have to let the boss know. Where's the bag?'

'Release my father and take us both to his office, and I'll tell you.' Naively she thought she had bought Salem another half hour.

99

7

Salem was home, but wished he wasn't. His mother had calmed down a little, but it was only just under control.

'I still don't understand why you have to go.'

'Mother if I tell you, you will get hurt, and I have enough pain to bear.'

'But, will you never be able to come back?'

He looked at her and his face softened. 'Of course I'll come back, but it may be a while.'

'Where're you going now?'

'I can't tell you, because I don't really know.'

'Does Tariq?'

'He probably knows the first part of the route.'

He picked up his bag and held her. She would not let him go and he had to release her fingers gently from his arms. He crossed the courtyard swiftly and found Tariq in the museum.

'One last look over the town!'

'Hurry, we have very little time.'

Once again Salem hung over the balcony above the city. On his left the snow still covered the mountain tops. The souk was bustling and storks had not ceased their endless search for food for the young perched precariously on the minaret. The unchanging scene briefly warmed his cold heart as he made his vow to return with Selwa.

God help her and Arbil when the bomb goes off! He knew there was nothing he could do about it. *We've got it wrong*, he thought, *you can't blame fate or stars, as the man wrote, it is within ourselves. I planted that bomb, not Allah.*

Tariq kicked the motor bike to life and away they were towards the mountains.

Salem leaned over and shouted: 'How long?'

'About an hour, then someone else takes over. Probably another hour after that.'

'Am I crossing by the bridge over the gorge?'

There was no reply as his words were lost in the wind. In any case it didn't matter; nothing mattered any more. He calculated it would be dark by the time he reached the border, which was good if he wished to survive. He really didn't care any more.

They'd turned off the main road and were heading into the mountains. The track ran out and Tariq dismounted. He indicated to Salem to go ahead along the narrow track. Salem nodded and proceeded. He heard footsteps behind him and assumed it was Tariq. Ten minutes later he reached a narrow ledge, high over the valley. He turned round.

His only companion was a complete stranger, who smiled reassuringly.

'Where's Tariq?'

'He said to say goodbye.'

Salem leaned wearily against the cold rock. 'So the old man was unable to bear the parting. What the hell does he expect me to do?'

'Come, we must be at the village in one hour.'

'What village?'

'I'm not sure it has a name any more, it's been deserted since the war started.'

'Which war?'

'This one. . . . It's next to the bridge. With a bit of luck the only ones there will be your guides into Iran.'

'I'm not sure I want to go with them.'

The guide looked at him sympathetically. 'I know, but just because we are the ones who face death doesn't mean you have to go looking for it.'

He placed his hand gently on Salem's shoulder and guided him round the ledge until the path took them away again into the valley, always east and, for Salem, a hopeless and pointless journey.

They reached the village at 5.30. The sun was heading home but Salem estimated they had half an hour's light and suggested they moved through the village and wait amongst the rocks at the base of the mountain which towered above. He knew the guides would come from that direction and they would be able to spot any pursuers.

'What happened to these people?'

'The President invited them to move, he even sent transport.'

'You mean they were rounded up and taken off south.'

'Yes, a few boys escaped and are now with us in the mountains,' he gestured with his hands towards the north. 'I'm told this happened to all the villages around the border.'

'That's right, he's trying to destroy us. If there's any arguing, they simply gas the place. Consequently, most people move.'

'Don't they realise there are four million of us. Twenty altogether, if you include Turkey, Iran and Russia. He's going to kill us all?'

'Well, one of his heroes, Hitler, managed to kill that many Jews.'

'Yes, but he was organised and the world probably didn't know what was going on. They do here.'

'Yes, but nobody cares about us. When you consider our history's been written down for a thousand years and we've only had a country for three, I think you can safely conclude we are on our own.'

'Why can't they simply let us get on with our lives? After all, nobody else would want these mountains and we don't threaten anyone any more. The only time we fight is amongst ourselves.'

'Well at the moment it is because of oil and in a hundred years it will be something else.'

'So what do you do besides guided tours of the mountains of Kurdistan?'

'I used to teach history . . . ours, not theirs. Then they shot my wife and child. They said it was an accident.'

Salem could see the matter-of-fact statement was an attempt to disguise a man's life ruined, his purpose spent.

'I'm sorry.'

The guide shrugged. 'We all have tales to tell. Revenge is not that sweet and really changes nothing. I've grown weary of killing Iraqi soldiers, after all most of them would rather be at home with their families. They're only here out of fear. I know they would run away if there was a real enemy. After all, considering they had no opposition in the air, they're still unable to beat an army which rose from the ashes of Khomeni's revolution.'

'Yes, the only thing they're really good at is killing their own people, particularly if they're unarmed.'

'Well maybe . . . one day the world will be shocked enough to ignore this sacrosanct thing they call national borders and send someone in to shoot the bastard. After all, even the Sunnis want to get rid of him, and the Iraqi national borders are recent, artificial and were settled by the British in the Cafe Royale. After all, there is nowhere else in the world which has straight lines for national borders.'

'You're wrong in one thing. There are a group who don't want to get rid of Sodom, it's the Tikriti Mafia.'

'Yes, but they go down with him.'

'Well, we're both dreaming.'

'Oh, I don't know. When you look at Saudi Arabia and Kuwait who've only been around a few years . . . they've managed to survive, despite having repressive archaic regimes, despite being spoilt brats who've never done a day's work. You could be sure the West would ensure their survival. They need the oil.'

'But we have oil.'

'No, Sodom has oil.'

The guide gestured him to silence. They both listened. The sun was setting behind the village. They both heard it together. Helicopters.

'We should move towards the border.'

'No we're ordered to wait here. There could be an ambush at the bridge. They have to check it out.'

They watched as the three helicopters circled the village then swooped and hovering briefly squatted in a cloud of dust on the far side of the ruined houses. A small grove of oaks hid them from the watchers in the rocks.

Salem watched with a thumping heart as a slight figure appeared between the trees in the village. He knew immediately who it was, even in the gathering gloom. Everybody walks differently.

8

At around 4.30 England, as promised, meandered down the Embassy drive to the gate. There was no sign of anyone searching cars nor of Mary. She arrived five minutes later.

'Have you been waiting long?'

'Since the time we agreed to meet.' He was colder than usual, because he was missing the last hour's drinking. For him, the final sacrifice.

'Well, shall we go or not?'

'May as well now.'

They drove in silence through the dusty streets of Baghdad towards the souk. Mary wanted to look for some gifts to take to Mayo. This would be her last chance. She stopped the car.

'Listen, let's make the most of it, eh.'

'Okay.'

He took her hand and they wandered through the narrow alleyways, flanked by gold and silver shops, spice and suit shops, carpet and copper shops; lots of stock where the majority of the customers had no funds.

'Did you hear what happened to Selwa?'

'No.'

'Someone saw her being driven off by the security people. Something to do with Salem.'

He thought for a moment and decided there was nothing

he could do to help her.

'Bernie the bomb, at the Embassy said that they were searching vehicles.'

'Yes, they looked at the ones in the hospital car park, but I didn't see anyone at the apartment block. And certainly no one has been near yours because it was parked round the back.'

'Well, probably nothing to it. Let's go and look at some carpets. Do you know this is the best place to buy Iranian carpets? But you have to be careful how you ask for them, because they're not supposed to sell them.'

'Do you know anything about them?'

'Only that it's something to do with the number of knots. But if you are paying in Dinars, probably they are all worth buying.'

She didn't buy any carpets, reckoning they wouldn't last in Mayo. He pointed out that the shopkeepers often let them out in the streets for vehicles to run over them. She reckoned then she couldn't carry them.

England thought of the group back at the Embassy accelerating to their climax and wondered if he would be able to catch them up at the villa, next station on their alcoholic Via Dolorosa, a phrase he loved from Conrad.

'Let's have a look at the silver.'

He consulted her watch, since he never carried one – 5.30.

'I need to get back at the hospital to see someone fairly soon.'

She recognised the familiar tune which signalled the last waltz on the shopping expedition, and thought at least he'd sacrificed one hour for her.

'Just for a few minutes?'

'Okay.'

It was all rather pointless as he tapped his foot whilst Mary bought a few bits of silver in her favourite shop. With pictures of long lost Empire heroes fading away in the sunlight, shaking hands with the owner who would outlive them all, but only just. He never discussed politics, particularly with Englishmen whose only admirable quality, particularly those in the service of their country was to be rather good at disguising their ignorance.

At least this one didn't talk down to him and he shook hands with the blonde girl, who had given him dreams on several occasions, with enthusiasm. After all it was his only sale that week.

They walked back to the car. He tossed a Dinar to the old dignified gentleman leaning on a stick, who proclaimed he'd guarded it with his life whilst they had been away. Recovering fast, England opened the passenger door for Mary and helped her up the high step. He lifted the bonnet to see if anything looked different, not that he knew anything about engines, but he'd learnt a little in Ulster. He got down on his knees and looked under the vehicle. Nothing.

'Why did you do that, you never bothered before?'

'I'm just a little worried about Salem, particularly with the Selwa thing this afternoon.'

'I don't believe he'd do anything to harm us.'

'No, but he might be under pressure from home. He did tell me he was leaving Iraq for good.'

'What!'

'Yes, he said it this morning.'

'But why?'

'I don't know. I suppose I should have pressed him on it.'

'No, that would have been the English thing to do.'

He looked sideways at her and seeing her smile he laughed too and leaned over to kiss her. Her response was less than he'd hoped for.

'What's the problem now?'

'Your session in the Embassy.'

He started the car, having surveyed the petrol and oil levels and eased the Patrol into the heavy Thursday evening traffic.

'We should have gone to the lakes.'

'Still not too late. I thought you wanted to stay her for your last weekend.'

'I've still got a few days.'

'Okay, let's go them, but I must stop at the hospital first. I need to see that little girl from Basra and cancel the squash.'

Dusk was falling as he parked in the open space at the side of the hospital next to the mortuary (spare parts still awaited). The space backed onto several long gardens running towards the apartment block. It being Thursday night, there were no other vehicles. Mary climbed down.

'I'll go and start packing. . . .'

'Okay, won't be long.'

He watched as she walked along the dusty road towards the apartment block.

He waved to the guard and entered the side door of the hospital. Mary was half way along the road when she remembered the silver in the glove compartment. She forced herself to go back for it as, despite his facade of security consciousness, England usually forgot to lock the car, and she had no more Dinars.

*   *   *

England stood at the end of the bed and gazed down at the small, pale face lying on the pillow. The father looked up at him.

'Hello doctor, it's kind of you to come in.'

'Just wanted to make sure she was comfortable before I go for the weekend.'

'I appreciate it anyway.'

'I'll just go and tell Sister to make sure she's got plenty of painkillers.'

They shook hands.

The Sister looked steadily at him from behind the desk. 'Yes, Doctor.'

He hesitated. 'Do you know what happened to Selwa?'

She coloured slightly. 'I . . . I told the security officer that your Kurdish patient was up to something in the car park last night. He was near one of the Patrols.'

Suddenly England realised.

He raced to the door as the siren came closer and closer.

9

Selwa shivered as the helicopter flew north. They'd not bothered to give her any warm flying clothing, just flung her in the cabin and took off. She was also soaking below, as she'd been unable to hold on any longer. She was sure they would shoot her father as soon as she had done as they'd asked, but at least he had time to plead his case, whilst she betrayed Salem.

'We want him alive, your job is to persuade him to come with you. We'll arrange for the two of you to go to Europe together as soon as he tells what he's been up to.'

Her father had, of course, dismissed this with contempt when she told him. He knew their only goal was their own survival and they were at severe risk if they failed to stop whatever was about to happen, even if Sodom was not personally involved. He knew he would die, whatever happened, and concentrated his mind on trying to find a way out for his beloved daughter.

What a mess, he should have stopped it right at the beginning. Anyway, too late now. Besides he was weary and disorientated from the beating they had given him. Not for information, because he had nothing to give, just to influence his daughter. What bastards, and he was one of them, even if he rationalised it by telling himself he was not personally responsible. The fact is that if enough people had the courage to say no at the same time, Sodom would have gone.

They were given five minutes together.

'What can I do, Daddy!'

'Nothing, nothing at all. I can't see any way anyone of us can get out of this, including your boy.'

'Oh Daddy, I'm so sorry.'

'Young people fall in love. I'm just so sorry you'll not be able to enjoy it, even for a while.'

'But they promised.'

'Yes, I know. That was just to get you to go. I concentrated everything at trying to think of some way out, but we're all three trapped. If you bring him back, I may live. That's all.'

'Then I have no choice but to go along.'

He kissed her gently as they dragged her away. She did not hear the shot, as she was already airborne. Neither could she hear the conversation in the cockpit.

'What the hell is this all about?'

'God knows.'

'Must be hot if we're flying so close to the border with that bastard on the same route.'

'Well, keep your eyes open, you remember what happened to the other relative last year when they crashed in that non-existent sandstorm.'

'I had a good look around, this really must be a last minute thing because they took none of the usual precautions. It'll be practically dark by the time we get there. No landing lights, no radar, no bugger all.'

The flight droned steadily on. They avoided the large town, sweeping instead along the western edge of the foothills. Once they heard the crackle of gunfire, but then that was normal here. The Flight Commander's voice came over the headphones:

'Estimate 20 minutes to landing. Follow me over the village, but keep your distance. I'll land first, then the girl,

111

and then our other guest. Acknowledge.'

They acknowledged. There was no problem with the flying; they were the best, although increasingly disillusioned with their lot. They'd several times discussed flying elsewhere.

'This wouldn't be a bad time to go? We've got the girl.'

'But who is she?'

'I don't know.'

'Well, we're obviously going to pick up someone else, or drop her off.'

'You mean like we dropped those others off from 2,000 feet?'

'No, they want her alive. That's why those bastards from the Guard are here.'

'Well, we've only got 10 minutes to make up our minds. But don't forget your family.'

*　　*　　*

Behind, Selwa was desperately trying to get her thoughts in some sort of order. Her first was the hope that Salem would be long gone. She knew he would need help to cross the border, but in her heart she knew darkness would be his other companion and that he was almost certainly waiting near the bridge. She knew there would be a few moments whilst she was given time to talk him back. How would he react? Scar-face leaned over her. She could smell last night's garlic. He shouted over the sound of the engine.

'When we land, you get out and walk towards the village, we'll be right behind you.'

'We don't even know if he's there.'

'He'll be there.'

'He won't move if he sees you.'

'We know that. Just do as you're told.'

'And my father?'

'Oh, he's probably home by now.'

112

He avoided her eyes and she knew that her only hope now was to save Salem. She felt the helicopter bank. How easy just to have gone with it and thrown herself through the door which was open now. The machine settled on the ground.

Her shoulder was gripped and she was bundled out onto the sand. Behind her the blood red sun was huge and slipping away. Above the mountain loomed its snowy peak, pink and cold. Where was Salem? Please God, he was already across the bridge. She stumbled through the trees and into the deserted village. Already the ruins were dark and shapeless. The unmade road through the centre was muddy and she picked her way carefully to the far end of the village, and looked towards the mountains. Keep walking, keep walking! Maybe if she could put enough distance between her and the butchers, there'd be a chance to run. Salem must have people with him.

10

Above the village Salem watched her progress through the trees and his heart seemed to fill his chest as she reached the last house. He could see her pale, beautiful face lifted towards him as if in prayer to the god of the mountain. He could see every feature through his guide's binoculars. He scanned the village, no sign of the rest of the party. They must be waiting in the trees.

'Who the hell is that?'

'A friend of mine.'

The professor of history looked across at him. 'You must go towards the bridge. I'll cover you. They won't know we're here. They're only guessing you're still around.'

Salem rested his forehead on his arms and said nothing.

'You must go,' urged his companion. 'If they catch you, it's your uncle, the boys in Baghdad, me, everybody.'

'If I go it's her, and I love her.'

'But there's no way you and she can get out of this.'

Salem looked again through the binoculars. Selwa was outlined by the orange sun. She brushed her hair away from her face, a gesture too much.

'I can't leave her to them.'

He handed the binoculars to his guide. 'I'm going down.'

'Wait! She's started walking. Let her come as far as possible. They won't shoot her until you appear.'

Selwa had seen the glint of glass and her whole being was

114

suddenly concentrated on reaching the rocks. She started to run, expecting any moment to feel the blow to her spine which would end it. Don't move Salem. They're not going to shoot me. How many men have you got? She'd lost her bearings. It was practically dark as she reached the edge of the rocks. Suddenly she saw a silhouette against the darkening skies, he leapt down a scree slope towards her.

'Salem my darling, stay there,' she screamed.

He slipped on the wet rock, and out of control, struck a sharp edged rock to her left.

The fountain of blood from his neck was subsiding as she reached him. His carotid had burst, as the doctor had warned him long ago when he refused further surgery. The hole in his neck had filled and she turned him on his side. He opened his eyes and smiled.

'We reached the mountains.'

'Yes my darling.'

His expression changed. He was near. She knelt to listen.

'Bomb. Doctor.'

She looked up. They were all around, staring at her.

'What did he say?'

'Something about a bomb, and a doctor.'

'Let's go.'

'What if there are more of them?'

'We'd know by now. Let's go. We have to get through to Baghdad, and there'll still be time. Bring the body.'

There were two bodies carried back to the village. Selwa had collapsed. As they were laid side by side, only the occasional small movement of her chest distinguished her from Salem. Both were covered in blood, but only he was at peace. Her hell was just beginning.

The Commander in the lead helicopter was speaking calmly into his throat microphone.

'We have the boy, or what's left of him. The only thing we have is a bomb and a doctor. We've got to get airborne. I don't know who is watching. This message at 6.09. Over and out.'

*   *   *

The convoy screamed across Baghdad. The best guess had been the Englishman's car which had been the only one not accounted for and assumed to be at Thatha, although a search there had been negative. Those drunken bastards at the Embassy had confirmed him shopping and then heading home. They'd sort out the protocol of bursting into the Embassy bar later. To hell with them. They're scared to upset us anyway, in case we stopped buying from them. They haven't even had the guts to defend that guy we put in jail for bribing the Mayor of Baghdad, even though he didn't, and the boss wanted rid of the Mayor. The President's personal bodyguard Commander was uneasy as these thoughts raced through his mind. He was on a hiding to nothing. No time, no precise information, and no excuse for failure.

They rounded the corner by the museum and into the hospital car park. The Commander stepped out of his car and was lifted off his feet.

11

They arrived together. Each knew the other without having met. The crater was some fifty feet across and, in the gloom, bottomless.

The mortuary had finally expired. The following week the spare parts arrived.

The Iraqi and the Englishman stood side by side, staring down into the black.

'Was yours the only car?'

'As far as I know. It's Thursday night, there was nobody else around.'

'Nobody?'

'Well, my. . . . girlfriend was walking back to the apartments, but that was a good five minutes ago.'

'Then perhaps we've been lucky.'

Men with torches arrived, followed by vehicles with search lights. Parts of the Patrol were found on the main road, two hundred yards away.

'We'll need to talk to you.'

'I know, but I must go back to the apartment first.'

The Commander looked at him suspiciously but, seeing no guile and sensing an increasing foreboding, nodded.

'These men will go with you,' indicating to England what seemed like a small army.

'There's no need, I'm not going anywhere, besides I have nothing for you.'

'You have ten minutes.'

England raced along the road to the apartments and took the steps two by two to the second floor. Mary was not in 2C where he, and they, lived. Maybe she'd gone to her official flat on nine, since most of her things were kept there in case there was a raid. The lift, as usual, took an age, then another to reach the top of the building. He raced along the balcony to the corner apartment and hammered on the door.

'It's open.'

He flung himself through the door.

'Where's Mary?'

'I thought she was with you.'

'Has she not been back at all?'

'No, and why did the whole building shake just now?'

'The Kurds blew up my car, but Mary had already left to come here.'

Their eyes met and she looked down. England took the nine flights down in nine strides and limped back along the road to the hospital, trailed by his escort. Half way along, he met the Commander.

'Doctor, I'm so sorry.'

There was really nothing left to take to Mayo, she had obviously just reached the glove compartment, but he knew her shoe.

He held it in his hands as he sat on the crater's edge, staring into Hell. He felt a light touch on his shoulder and looked up into Selwa's pale, bruised face, harshly lit by the searchlights.

'So we both lost.'

'But we weren't even in the game.'

118

PART III
REQUIEM

1

And so down the long diminishing years to the despair of Autumn, he was suddenly back in Baghdad. Zoo night at the Foreign Correspondents' Club, Ice House Street, Hong Kong, last outpost of the Empire, soon to be handed back to another bunch of murderers, the old stags in Beijing, defending their territory against the march of time.

Two shows were in progress, one around the bar, where all the men have a past, and none of the women have a future, or maybe it's the other way round, and the other on the screen where CNN's version of the world told England that Bushbaby, with Major Minor and Le petit Francois, were bombing the hell out of Baghdad in the name of freedom, and the price of petrol at the American pumps. They ended up liberating the wrong country.

The new world disorder unveiled under Bert's baleful eye. The era of peace, unless you had the misfortune to live in Rangoon, or Somalia, or Sarajevo or Armagh, or about twenty other places where the ugly face of nationalism was again on the rise. When will they ever learn?

So where was peace? England had tried many bars in many towns. Of all the crumbling institutions of his English youth, only the Bridge at Audlem had survived intact. He shared his sons' and daughter's world weariness and despair, for they had no example to follow, least of all from him. The Christian Era was in its twilight years, especially in Merrie England where simpering Bishops spent all their time deciding how many prefer the boys and whether to let the girls in. The spoiled Royal brats had put paid to another, since institutions only survive if someone believes in them and who can believe in a sour godmother who is determined to hang on to every penny of her inherited wealth whilst her country goes to the dogs? England was now one theme park, clinging to former glories, making nothing, encouraged by a strident Amazon, to selfish greed. A place where babies died on the waiting list and young men died for a frozen southern island of sheep and Maggie's re-election. Young blades in red braces were the heroes of the age. The only problem was the boom was all on paper and the hopes and fears of all those years were met only in dreams, then vanished with the dawn of the new decade when the account was rendered.

Hong Kong, the only boom town left in the "Western" world. Hong Kong, where in spite of, or because of, total lack of government, or government by overpromoted Gweilos who could barely run Accrington, greed was not only still good, but mandatory. Hong Kong, where a rather pathetic old gentleman from the Foreign Office, with half a chicken on his head, spent his time saying over and over again that he "did hope everything would be alright", and that those nice chaps in Beijing were really rather trust-worthy after all. Then came a new man full of self promot-ing zeal who in a late surge of Colonial guilt, in the last five years of a one hundred and fifty year rule of total indiffer-ence, suddenly decided those in Hong Kong had to have democracy, when all they really wanted to do was be left alone as before, to make lots of money.

The Foreign Correspondents' Club, no longer with the best bog view in the world, but still the best bar in town. Pretension was discouraged, consequently the peacocks and peahens of the Hong Kong Club, the Ladies' Recreation

Club and other Colonial Institutions, tended to steer clear, particularly on Zoo night, when everyone knew their place.

At the North End, just past Claire's Shrine in Whisky Tangoland where sit the Redlips Brigade, broomsticks parked at the door. Whiskey Tango, Cathay Pacific East Hostess speak for their White Trash supervisors and there was no argument about that at the south end of the bar where various legals and the occasional illegal gathered. A dwindling band of Wizards of Oz and Nuz. Hong Kong is one of those places where if you wish to brief your Barrister, you go and see him in jail.

England watched with sinking heart as the Allies pulverised Baghdad, pictures from the Rasheed Hotel where the story began, where once again the meek inherited the scorched earth and Sodom lived to continue his butchery. Bushbaby had it wrong when he said Vietnam was over. Sodom lives because of Vietnam.

England reflected against the wall of sound on the long journey from Baghdad. He'd witnessed the Fall of Man in Athens, another town, another bar, Flanagan's, jewel of Glyfada, meeting place of all the great modern Greek philosophers, headquarters of the Greek national rugby team, who had been refused entry to the Hong Kong Sevens on the basis that they were the only team in Greece. This did not take away the pain of rejection. This was left to B52's and various concoctions presided over by the club captain, Handy Andy, who had trained his mixed bunch of Brits, Greek Australians (who had reverted to their Athenian ways after working hard down under) and the Americans from the airbase who, deprived of the real meat of American Football, opted for the next best thing. For the first time, England understood this wayward, generous naive Nation, here represented by something like their best. He had never understood how such a talented nation, in all Nobel fields, could come up with such a

123

limited choice for the highest office. Perhaps it was the era of the professional politician who had never had a proper job. Worse still he was probably a lawyer.

The Athens rugby pitch, sited at the end of the runway, was the only one England had ever played on with landing lights behind the goal posts. This added to the air of surrealism, of working German. England had discovered the indefinable quality that makes the world, rightly, fear them, for they still have a total belief that they are best. He'd met their President, by accident, and the only man in a quarter of a century who obviously knew more about most things than England would ever know.

He reflected on the contrast between a great man, a gentleman, and the self appointed characters of old Hong Kong British Adventurers who were so busy trying to be the centre of attraction that they never listened to anybody else's conversation, bullshit interruptus, spiritual development around upright posture stage.

The previous weekend England had journeyed south to attend the annual charity lunch of the Macau Gentlemen's Outing Association, an ageing band of hopefuls, who hoped to retain their youth by the new craze of regular jogging. The only difference in their case, was that the Association rules demanded that the exercise be taken in the horizontal position, accompanied by one of the local lovelies. Beautiful they are, full of smiles despite their desperate country, where twenty families own ninety per cent of the land and corruption has destroyed all hope for the talented.

Here was the Red Rooster Hideaway, appropriately located in Conception Street and the nearest thing to a Mayo Bar, east of the Shannon. The only difference was that the Red Rooster had no Guinness and Mayo Bars do not have twenty or so dark beauties sitting waiting for you at the Bar. Decor wise, however, the bars were indistinguishable, down to the ancient jukebox which required the occasional kick. Jinglebells, a fellow Welsh choirboy, had demonstrated this only a week ago, and managed to smash a bottle of gin instead, by kicking the bar. The affair was discretely handled. They doubled all the bar bills.

Back in Hong Kong, the boys were ready to look after the 80,000 or so Filipinas who earned an equal amount as their Manila bar sisters with less endowment, as a maid. Hong Kong Land had tried to ethnically cleanse the maids' Sunday playground but had withdrawn under threat.

So where was Peace in all this? Does anybody really recover from pelvic-led, western love, particularly where the partner has already taken on the American Mediterranean Fleet during a two week Balearic holiday, seen them off and still had time for a few locals? Also the first cut was already made. He'd left the Welsh choirboys because it was full of jewelers, Bible bearers and Exhorters and consequently did not make a joyful sound despite producing the best Amen, east of Suez.

At last he plucked up the courage to make the pilgrimage.

The Cottage lay amongst the pines, four square with a peat fire. Red door. It looked down to the ribbon of the Moy, as it roared under the arched stone bridge that took the road to Swinford. Far, far away in the misty west loomed Croagh Patrick, where the faithful ascend on their knees. It's said in Swinford, that if you can see Croagh Patrick, it's a foin day. England had never seen Croagh Patrick, not even after climbing above the cottage to the small fields, each of which was named. Below, away from the bridge, was the bottomless, black lake alongside the little stone church, sturdily perched on a green mound, amongst the silver birch, whose leaves shimmered in the moist air.

The road to the lonely cemetery was arrow straight from the main road between Swinford and Foxford. He and the stonewalled field were entirely alone in this world. He found her gravestone and sat beside it. He cleaned away the encroaching turf and placed the lilies of the valley across her name. The air was warm and he was tempted to lie down and stay there for ever. Nothing mattered.

He was woken by the soft rain and sat up. Across the valley, towards Westport, he saw the clouds part and a great ray of setting sun outlined the bulk of Croagh Patrick. Behind a rainbow coloured the black angry sky. He thought he heard her voice but it was only God's tears. Whether of joy or sorrow, he did not know, but this being the poets' land, he heard the small boy whisper urgently to his newly arrived sister, when at last left alone. 'Hurry up and tell me what God looks like, I'm starting to forget.'

All men make mistakes, but a good man yields when he knows his course is wrong and repairs the evil. The only sin is pride.